EARTH'S SECRET
EARTH'S MAGIC
BOOK FIVE

EVE LANGLAIS

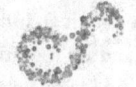

Earth's Secret © 2023 Eve Langlais

Cover by Addictive Covers © 2023

Produced in Canada

Published by Eve Langlais

http://www.EveLanglais.com

E-ISBN: 978 177 384 4701

Print ISBN: 978 177 384 4718

ALL RIGHTS RESERVED

This book is a work of fiction and the characters, events and dialogue found within the story are of the author's imagination and are not to be construed as real. Any resemblance to actual events or persons, either living or deceased, is completely coincidental.

No part of this book may be reproduced or shared in any form or by any means, electronic or mechanical, including but not limited to digital copying, file sharing, audio recording, email and printing without permission in writing from the author.

PROLOGUE

THE FLAMES WERE SO PRETTY DANCING ALL AROUND HER. Mesmerizing too. The young girl hugged her knees and rocked as they flickered, keeping her warm—a good thing since they'd long burned away her clothes.

As she basked in the heat that didn't singe her skin, one word kept whispering around her, as if the flames themselves spoke.

Forget.

Forget.

Forget.

Forget what?

The word repeated, over and over again, growing fainter and fainter as the fire ran out of things to burn.

The young girl shivered as her skin, exposed to the night air, lost its cocoon of warmth. Only her bum remained comfortable sitting atop the hot coals.

She slept until she was woken by a shout.

"There's someone over here!" A crunch of boots

opened her eyes, and she beheld a fireman wearing a helmet that covered his whole head. He shouted, "Holy mother earth, it's a child sitting in the coals. Someone call the CA. I think she's one of theirs."

The man didn't come any closer but he did crouch. "Hey, little girl. What are you doing here?"

She cocked her head but didn't reply because she didn't know.

"Do you have a name? I'm Dennis."

Her mouth opened—*Forget. Forget. Forget.*—She struggled against the whispery voice in her head to whisper, "Marissa."

The only thing she could remember. That, and her age.

How old are you? She almost said I don't know, only to see her hand whip up flexing all of its fingers and her thumb.

Age and name. The only things she remembered despite how many times she was questioned or how many people with mellow voices asked. One of them even had her hold a doll and said, "Who's your doll's mommy? Does she have a name?"

Her reply? *Dolls aren't real.*

Not to mention, she might only be five, but she knew what they tried to do. They just wouldn't believe her when Marissa said she didn't know.

It didn't help that no one ever came forth to claim her. Her DNA never matched anything on file.

That little girl grew up never knowing her roots, although the fact she inherited magic didn't come as a surprise, given how they found her. Her magic, while present, didn't get a boost until the goddess Hekate accepted her application to be her disciple. All the most powerful witches had a god benefactor. The nicer ones chose Mother Earth. The mean ones worshipped the devil.

Hekate sat somewhere in between. A powerful being who specialized in magic but only rarely interacted with the world or her followers, although she answered when Marissa asked, *Do you know where I came from?* The goddess replied, *Great care was taken to hide your origin.*

Great care by who?

Decades later, the woman still wondered.

CHAPTER 1

"We've got a thirteen thirty-one on Maple Street." CA code for cryptid causing trouble.

The call came in mid-shift, interrupting my reading time. Don't judge. While at times my job as a Cryptid Agent—AKA police for supernatural folk—could be busy, most of the time the highlight of the day involved herding fairies out of the flower shop or reminding gnomes they couldn't get naked and bathe in sprinklers on people's front yards. I especially hated it when I showed up and they'd gone from naked soaping to fucking in the middle of the grass. Some things couldn't be unseen.

"Anyone close by?" dispatch asked.

Since I happened to be literally a block away, I buzzed in. "This is Agent Smith. I'm in the area and will check it out."

"I'll see who's close by for backup," Horace stated,

the guy running dispatch since Evangeline went on maternity.

"Don't bother. I'm good. If it's too much to handle, I'll give you a shout." Unlike other agents who patrolled, I currently worked alone. I'd not yet been assigned a new partner since the shakeup at my office.

In the last few months, a ton of people had been fired and, in some cases, even charged. My old boss had been the worst. Turned out she'd been colluding with an evil witch and abetted in innocents getting slaughtered. The witch had since been killed, and as for my boss? She now sat in a cell waiting for trial. Karma in action.

Other agents got swept up on charges of dereliction of duty because they knew what happened and didn't report or stop it. A few, like Ralph—the asshole I'd been reluctantly paired with—were discovered to have been taking bribes to look the other way from cryptids behaving badly. I couldn't say I was sad to see the lazy fucker go. Ralph should have never been given a badge.

Given the shakeup left our CA office short-staffed, and given I was a senior staffer with actual magic, they'd opted to let me work alone for the moment—until some new agents could be transferred or recruited. I hoped that took a long time. I quite enjoyed working solo. My car stayed clean—no more fast-food wrappers all over the place or the smell of the burps that came after. No dealing with assholes who treated me like I couldn't hold my own because I didn't have a sausage between my legs. A witch didn't need a man with a gun to protect her. I'd zap any threats myself, thank you very much.

According to the address, the location hosted a storage unit place. I parked outside the closed gate by the main office. As I stepped out, I didn't sense anything untoward. Sometimes the stench of a crime in progress hit you with eye-watering results, like that time I checked out a ghoul preying on graveyards. No mistaking the putrid decay in that case.

A woman, her hair bleached to the point I'd think twice about even brushing it, emerged from the square building. Her wild eyes went well with her harried expression. "We're closed," she barked.

I flashed my badge. "I'm Agent Marissa Smith from the Cryptid Authority. We got a call about a disturbance."

"Thank the baby Jesus you're here. You have to do something about the monster."

Humans had a thing for calling anything that didn't look like them monsters. Most of the time, the cryptids in question were benign. The dangerous ones weren't allowed into populated areas.

"What can you tell me about the intruder? Do you know where it came from? Are you sure it's still on the premises?"

"It was inside one of the storage units. I only found it by accident when I opened it to see what I could auction off for nonpayment."

Sounded like it might be a case of an illegal cryptid

pet. It happened. People bought them on the black market and either kept them as status symbols or used them in fights—or for rare ingredients.

"Did you recognize the type of creature?" I asked.

She shook her head. "No idea what it is, but it sure is ugly. Reminds me of my great-grandpa when he was on his death bed with the big C. Gaunt body but giant head!" She held out her hands in what surely had to be an exaggeration.

"You say it was inside one of the storage units?"

At my query, she nodded. "Unit 5C. One of our longest-running clients. Always paid on time until about six months ago."

Six months... Hunh. That was when all the shit with the witch and the corruption at my office went down.

"Is the creature still inside the unit?"

"I don't know. Once I saw it, I took off running. Thought my heart was going to burst." She put a hand to her chest.

"You have cameras?" I queried, seeing one aimed at the entrance.

"Yes, but they're not working. I keep meaning to get them fixed."

Shame. It might have given me an idea of what I dealt with.

I walked to the gate and eyed it. Easy to climb even with the barbed wire sprouting from the top. There was a good chance the intruder hadn't remained confined.

I glanced at the owner over my shoulder. "You said it reminded you of your great-grandpa. So, humanoid in shape?"

Her head bobbed. "Yes. It looked like an old crotchety man with a gigantic head. And when it hissed at me, it had sharp teeth."

Add in the fact she'd found it inside a storage unit and I had a feeling I knew what we dealt with. A Spriggan, known for their obsessiveness in guarding what they considered treasures. Not common for this side of the ocean, given they were of Cornish origin. Most likely illegally imported. They tended to be cheaper to feed than paying for actual security.

"I'll need to get inside." I inclined my head at the gate.

"Alone?" She eyed me and pursed her lips. Even with my own sex, I got disrespected.

"This is what I do, ma'am." I refrained from rolling my eyes.

"Okay, but if anyone asks, I'm gonna swear on a stack of Bibles that you're doing it willingly. I ain't getting sued or arrested because you think you're some kind of super woman."

Did I really look that inept?

I blamed the hair. Bright pink and determined to remain that shade no matter how many attempts I made to bleach or dye it.

"You won't be blamed if I get hurt," I sighed. "Now would you please open the gate?"

"Whatever. Your funeral," she muttered as she

went back into the building. A moment later, the gate clanked as it rolled open, revealing asphalt that branched between the long single-story buildings with roll-up doors. The siding, a bright yellow, contrasted with the blue of the various units. I saw no sign of anything untoward. Could be the cryptid remained inside the unit it guarded.

As I took a step into the enclosed area, the woman emerged. "Aren't you going to put on a vest or grab a gun?"

"I've got something better than that." I lifted my hand, and magic shimmered into place around me, forming a shield more durable than any Kevlar.

"Feckin' witch," muttered the woman.

A rather rude thing to say given I'd come to help her out, but I was used to humans denigrating those of us with power. It had to be hard knowing they would never be blessed with magic and the potential for greatness. A bitchy thing to think, perhaps, but having grown up being bullied for being different, I no longer gave a fuck.

I'd barely gone three paces when the gate rattled along its track, shutting me in. Some might have been pissed the owner left me with no quick exit. Me, though, I thought it smart. I'd hate for the cryptid to slip out and make my job harder.

Given I had no idea of the layout, I walked straight, head tilted, every single one of my senses scanning. I heard nothing. Saw nada. Smelled zilch. Not even a tingle of magic whispered past me.

The units had letters and numbers on the outside of them, which led to me trying to remember the unit the woman had mentioned, which I'd already forgotten. I could have returned to ask her, but she already thought me incompetent and I had no intention of reinforcing her shitty opinion. Besides, the place wasn't that big. Surely I'd run into the cryptid at one point.

I kept walking and murmured, "Come out, come out, wherever you are."

At a cross-section, I glanced left, just in time to catch the blur that dove at me. As my body moved to avoid, I took in details of my attacker. Slight figure, body wrinkled and grayish in tone, head massive and sprinkled with greasy strands of hair. Spriggan confirmed.

Now it should be noted, as a CA agent I swore to try and do no deadly harm. We weren't in the business of killing cryptids but rather had a mandate to capture. All that to explain why I didn't blast the Spriggan into tiny meat chunks despite the fact it would have taken a bite out of me.

Instead, I sidestepped its attack and, as it rushed past, cast out my hand to wrap the creature in a magical fist that it couldn't escape. Once the Spriggan realized it had been caught, it screeched and flailed, its head and lower part of its legs the only things able to move.

"No. No. No," it shrieked.

"Behave," I chided. Spriggans had rudimentary

speech comprehension. Usually. This one didn't appear to be listening, given it kept struggling. "Calm your ass down. I'm not here to harm you. I'm Agent Smith with the Cryptid Authority."

It hissed, "Release us."

"No can do. You don't belong this side of the big pond. You are under arrest for being here illegally." The fact the Spriggan most likely had been smuggled in didn't matter. Certain species were prohibited from relocation, especially the harmful varieties.

"No go," it stubbornly insisted.

"Be pissed all you want. It doesn't change the facts. You are going to come with me to the CA precinct. In good news, once we've figured out where you were snatched from, you might be returned so long as you haven't committed any violent crimes." Because if it had, then it would be headed to a super-prison instead. We had them scattered around the globe. Maximum-security buildings, often partially buried underground or in mountains, with insanely complex magical safeguards in order to prevent the escape of those deemed too dangerous for society.

The Spriggan paused its thrashing for a moment and stared at me. Its mouth opened wide in a grin as it murmured, "Yummy pink candy."

Gross. But not as gross as its hard-on.

"Ew. Put that thing away."

"I gets to go first!" it crowed.

Odd thing to say until I realized there were two of them!

As the second Spriggan slammed into me from behind, I couldn't keep my balance and found myself pitching face-first. My shield kept me from getting a face full of asphalt; it also kept the claws at bay. I pushed more magic into it, heating my defense enough the Spriggan attempting to eviscerate me yelped and sprang away. However, my beefed-up shield and attack caused me to lose my hold on the first Spriggan.

Quickly, I shoved to my feet, annoyed at having been caught by surprise.

"Gonna adds you to our collection," hissed the first creature, who didn't run once released from my magical grip.

"I says we eats her," lisped the second.

And then a third I never noticed just had to chime in. "Breed her."

Oh hell to the no. Outnumbered, and with no time to call for help, I prayed to my goddess, even as I knew she might not answer.

Hekate wasn't like some of the other deities who reveled in being worshipped. She tended more to the aloof side and encouraged independence from her followers, which might explain why she had only a few.

To my surprise, she answered my call, not with words or encouragement though. My magical reservoir suddenly filled, the power tingling me head to toe, so much I almost burst with it.

"Oh, hell yeah," I murmured. "Let's go, you

fuckers."

As the trio of Spriggans suddenly barreled for me, thinking they could crush me by working in tandem, I took the magic brimming within and expelled it, forcing it outward in a wave that didn't just knock my assailants flat; it dented the storage units on either side.

Damn. My goddess truly had come through for me.

When the concussion of the magic wave faded, I swiftly moved to secure the cryptids before they could rouse from their daze. I bound their hands with strips of iron, rendering each Spriggan defenseless. Only then did I use my phone to call in.

"Gonna need the van for pickup," I declared, feeling rather proud of myself.

"On its way," Horace stated in reply.

While I waited for the paddy wagon to arrive, I sauntered past the damage, looking for the original unit that held the Spriggans. It proved easy to find. For one, it remained open. Two, it stank. And three, it held a litter of ugly little Spriggans that appeared to be feeding off the corpse of a woman with her stomach ripped open. Yikes. Looked like they'd been discovered just in time. The damage this many Spriggans might have caused if they got loose would have caused some serious PR nightmares with our CA office.

The hissing younglings were easily corralled, their tiny bodies too undeveloped yet to do more than express their displeasure.

With that finished, I peeked inside the unit,

wondering who in their right mind paid to house these creatures. To my surprise, while the front of the unit might be a mess, the back of it appeared untouched. A harder glance with my othersight—what I called looking past the real world to that of the esoteric—showed a shimmer of power. A curtain of magic protected stacks of boxes. Boxes I recognized, of sorts. The CA logo was stamped across them, and I had to wonder at their content. Confiscated goods stolen from our office? Personal files? Or junk that simply happened to be stored in some branded boxes?

Before I could find out, a commotion in the form of voices and gates rattling open indicated reinforcements had arrived.

I exited the storage unit to see Pablo and Felicia approaching, the former being honest enough to not be involved in the previous rot in our office and the latter a new hire. They were accompanied by the storage complex owner, who had her lips pursed in a mighty scowl.

"Your Spriggan problem has been neutralized," I informed her as she got within talking distance.

"You destroyed my place!" she shrieked. "I am going to sue."

Actually, she couldn't, as the CA had a government sanction to use whatever force necessary to subdue misbehaving cryptids.

"Insurance should cover the damage," I advised.

"If I had any!"

"In that case, go after the person who illegally

stored the Spriggans on your property." I tried to give her options, but she shot that one down as well.

"Hard to get money out of a dead-beat client," the woman grumbled, crossing her arms.

"I'm sure there's something that can be done." Pablo tried to soothe the irate owner and led her away.

Meanwhile, Felicia snorted. "Some people just don't know how to say thank you."

"No shit." I'd risked my life to help and all I got was grief—and not just from the owner of the storage units.

My new boss, a stern and grizzled former military advisor, Abe Kowalski, called me into his office and gave me a stern look as he said, "You took a big risk going in by yourself once you realized the dangerous situation."

"A danger I handled," I pointed out.

"Only because you got lucky," he barked. "And that's not acceptable. Protocol states, in the case of aggressive cryptids, an agent is to wait for backup unless there is imminent danger to themselves or civilians."

"I didn't know there was three of them."

"But you did suspect a Spriggan, correct?" At my nod, he continued to berate. "This office has been through too much shit lately for me to have to deal with the paperwork of an agent who thinks she's above the rules. I'm putting you on desk duty until we can find you a partner who will temper your vigilante ways."

"You're benching me? But I'm one of the best you have." I couldn't hide my shock.

"Exactly and we could have lost you today because you were cocky." Kowalski's lips turned down. "Trust me, I don't like doing this, but you've left me no choice."

He had a choice. He could let me do my job.

Instead, I got relegated to the basement.

CHAPTER 2

Being placed on desk duty sucked. Even worse, the punishment wasn't because I'd failed to do my job. I'd captured the Spriggans. Done so without loss of life and yet, instead of being commended, I'd been disciplined.

So unfair.

Some people might have pouted or whined, even yelled. Having been around the block a few times in my thirty-five years, I'd reached a maturity level that allowed me to accept my boss's decision without resorting to the stomping of my feet or quitting. Although I was tempted. Inaction didn't suit me.

As if being stuck inside the precinct didn't blow enough, I also didn't get to work on active case files. A part of me hoped I'd be able to prove a point by making a few calls, searching a few databases, and piecing together some clues to solve a crime. I was a damned good agent.

Instead of showing off my skills, I got sent to the basement to deal with the stash of boxes recovered from the storage unit. To my surprise, according to the info Kowalski messaged me, the criminal who stashed them turned out to be none other than my last boss. The crooked one. Apparently, rather than having old CA case files digitized, she'd chosen to steal and hide them away for no reason anyone could discern.

My task? To check every single one of those files against our databases before shredding them. If the file was missing online, then I got the lovely task of inputting them one by one. It should be noted, typing was not one of my strong points.

I grimaced as I entered the musty room with a single tiny—and dirty—window covered in bars. The boxes numbered seven in total and had been stacked in a corner. My workspace consisted of a dented metal table, a chair that appeared on its last legs, and an ancient computer. A sticky note beside it had log-in instructions.

I spent the first three days of my punishment bored out of my mind and annoyed. Turned out all of the records needed to be manually added to the database of cryptid crimes. My slow and painful hunt and peck at the keyboard meant each missing report took me ages to add. It didn't help the things I had to update were stupid.

Gnome stole a lawn ornament. Who cared? It happened a decade ago.

Fairies got drunk on fermented fruit. Again, a nothing burger.

A neighbor's dog pissed on a witch's roses and caused them to wilt. Why had anyone even bothered writing the complaint down?

On and on the list of petty crimes went, both a waste of paper and my time. None of these needed to be saved forever. I could have shredded them all and the world wouldn't have known the difference, especially since most of the case files went back decades.

The last box with the most mildew and rodent damage made me sigh. The chew and piss marks made the files more challenging to discern, and once I did, I could have screamed, as it was just more dumb shit—warlock made it rain Popsicle dicks for a Pride parade, a goblin stealing garbage cans, a child found in the ashes of a house that burned down. A little girl with pink hair and no last name.

I blinked and reread the last file in disbelief.

Holy fuck. The report was about me. I was that child. An orphan whose memories started the moment social services took me into custody. Despite trying everything—therapy, magic, even hypnosis—I couldn't remember anything of my past. Not even the fire.

As I'd aged and asked questions about my origin, the social workers blew me off, claiming the details about my rescue had been lost.

I hadn't believed them, so at eighteen, I'd signed up to become a Cryptid Authority agent, thinking I'd have access to more details about my rescue. However, it turned out they spoke the truth. The original case file had gone missing.

Until now.

I held it in my hand, a folder not very thick, as it contained only a few pages, and yet I trembled. Despite my curiosity, I found myself unable to flip from the first to the next page. Instead, I stared at the earliest known picture of me. Solemn-faced, my eyes too big for my face, my hair the same shocking pink of today. I wore an oversized shirt. Someone must have given me the one off their back to hide my nudity.

As my shock wore off, I pored over the details, sparse as they were.

My story began with a house fire, one already blazing hot and furious before the fire services even arrived on the scene. Given the inferno-like conditions, it was assumed no one survived. Meaning, they didn't risk anyone's life sending them in to look. Rather than waste a ton of time or resources, they let the flames peter out on their own.

Only once the smoke cleared did the investigating fire marshal notice a child sitting amongst the ashes. Hugging her knees, head pressed to them, her pink hair a curtain around her naked body.

Convinced the tyke must be cryptid, the fire marshal called in the Cryptid Authority, who swept in and bundled the little girl off for testing and questioning.

The blood and DNA samples labelled me as

human. At the time, I showed no evidence of being gifted in any way, nor did anything in my appearance set me apart, unless the pink hair and surviving the raging blaze counted. Since they couldn't identify me and no one stepped forward to claim me, the CA placed me in the foster care system, which, in my case, turned out to not be horrible. My foster parents were actually decent folk. Unlike others in the system, I didn't get shipped around and had a normal childhood if we ignored how I'd gotten orphaned in the first place.

According to the report, questions about my parents—who my family was—went unanswered. I couldn't explain a single thing. I didn't know or remember how I got there. I had no memories of parents or guardians, or anyone for that matter. Just my name.

The investigating agents lost interest in my case. It fizzled off to nonconclusive and then disappeared entirely. Until now.

I would have liked to have read more but for two things. One, the last few pages had gotten damp and were now stuck together, and two, my phone went off with a text from the boss.

My office. Asap.

Was that an *I'm-out-of-the-dog-house-come-see-me* or a *you're-about-to-be-on-my-permanent-shit-list* request?

Only one way to find out. However, first, given no one had a clue what hid in the boxes, I stashed the file about me in my oversized purse—which I carried not because I kept a shit-ton of girl stuff on me, but more because it acted as my lunch bag and was big enough for the books I liked to read when my shifts were slow.

As to those who would clutch their pearls at my minor theft, too bad. I didn't feel the slightest bit guilty. My file had already been lost for thirty years, and I doubted anyone gave a damn other than me. Besides, I didn't need anyone else knowing about my mysteriously fucked-up childhood.

I headed up from the dungeon to the main floor and exited into the bullpen, where it seemed everyone clustered around something. Or I should say, someone.

A tall man stood amidst the agents with his back to me, his hair a lustrous black with a blue sheen, his shoulders broad. Whoever he was, he had everyone enthralled. Me, I had a meeting with the boss to attend, so I stalked past to knock on Kowalski's door.

"Come in," barked my boss.

I entered to find Kowalski sitting behind his desk looking peeved, which, I should add, seemed to be his permanent expression.

"You wanted to see me, sir." I started with a respectful tone. I could always resort to freaking out later if he tried to punish me further.

"I did. Am I right to assume you'd like to get out of desk duty?"

"Hell yeah." I didn't even attempt to curb my enthusiasm.

"Good. Because I'm going to need all agents on deck."

"Has something happened?" I'd not heard of any problems; then again, I didn't have a ton of coworkers I chatted with. I tended to keep to myself.

"No issues yet, but it appears that one of the super prison escapees might be heading our way."

I well remembered the scandal from last year, as every CA office had gone on high alert for weeks, with good reason. A prison for the most dangerous cryptids had been destroyed, releasing a great number of its inhabitants. While some had been caught, many still remained at large.

"Any idea of what we're keeping an eye out for?"

"A chimera who was in captivity for more than three decades for crimes against humanity. As far as we know, she's not in town, but there's been a report of her popping up a few hours away."

A chimera? How rare. There were only a handful left in the world. What little I knew about their species stated they were usually adept at fire magic and could shift into a beast shape that varied. Some had wings. Others, three heads. I even recalled an image of one with a serpentine tail. The one other thing I knew? They were considered dangerous.

I did so love a challenge.

I barely contained my excitement as I asked, "You want me to see if I can scry for her?"

"Already been tried. She's wily and knows how to hide her tracks. All the CA expert could do was confirm that the chimera was in the area around the fires because she left behind traces of her essence."

Interesting. I didn't have the kind of powers to pick up specific cryptid essence from sites, otherwise I'd have been tempted to try it myself, just to get a beat on this woman.

Kowalski continued. "The only reason we even caught wind of her is because of the fires she's been causing. In the most recent one, she was actually caught by video surveillance breaking into a mobile phone store. It burned down right after. Given her propensity for arson, I'll want you to personally start investigating all nearby blazes to see if you can connect her to any of them, so we know if she's made it into town yet."

I didn't groan despite knowing most of the fires I'd be checking out would be benign in origin. Sometimes being a CA agent meant doing a bunch of dull and repetitive footwork in the hopes of finding a clue that would lead to the culprit. On the bright side, arsonists sometimes hung around to admire their handiwork, so it was possible I could end up making an arrest. "Am I apprehending, or is there a termination order?" While the Cryptid Authority did its best to arrest rather than kill, in some cases we had no choice. The lives of those we protected had to come first.

His eyes snapped up to meet mine. "You are not to approach the chimera under any circumstances. You are to investigate the fires, and if there happens to be a sighting of the chimera then you call for backup—call *me*. Do not speak to her. Do not give her a chance to speak to you. Their kind are tricksters and murderers and cannot be trusted."

"Yes, sir. On it, sir."

"Not quite yet, Smith. There is one more thing." Before Kowalski could tell me what that thing was, someone knocked on his door.

"Come in," called out my boss.

The stranger from the bullpen entered, even prettier from the front than the back. His native ancestry showed in his smooth tanned skin and dark eyes.

"Hey, Abe." The man greeted my boss with familiarity.

"Koda, glad you could be here on short notice." Kowalski stood and offered his hand for a shake.

"My pleasure to help."

I had a bad feeling about this, which my boss confirmed a second later.

"Agent Marissa Smith, say hello to your new partner, Agent Koda Whiteclaw."

"Partner?" I exclaimed. "I don't need a partner."

"You do if you want out of desk duty," my boss growled.

My lips pinched. I did want out. Still... I eyed the good-looking man. "Hold on... Koda Whiteclaw. I know that name."

"You should," my boss said. "He's the one who recently busted that underground pixie drug ring." They'd been selling their drunken glitter to humans, leading to a sharp increase in indecent exposure incidents. "He also tracked down the stolen beanstalk seeds." They'd been stolen from the museum, and there'd been fear they would be planted, giving the very ornery giants living in Cloud Plane over Earth access to the planet. They were apparently still pissed about the whole Jack-stealing-the-golden-goose incident.

"So he's the CA's super-agent darling. Good for him. I still don't want him as a partner."

"Oh, so you'd rather return to the basement?" Kowalski arched a brow.

"No." I didn't sulk, but only because I bit my inner lip. "He better not be as useless as my last partner." Not a really high bar given Ralph's only real skill? Knowing the locations of the best greasy spoons.

At my complaint, Koda Whiteclaw's lips split into a smile. "I'll do my best to not disappoint."

"How about you just stay out of my way?"

"I assure you I am quite capable."

I would have loved to argue that point, but I'd heard of him. Everyone had, hence why he had his own little fan club.

"This is non-negotiable, Smith. You will work with Agent Whiteclaw."

"If I must," I muttered. "Was that all?"

"Almost." My boss slid over a folder marked Classified. "I've already briefed Agent Whiteclaw on our chimera, but here's the official file."

I flipped it open and frowned at the slim sheaf within, most of it redacted. "You've got to be kidding.

It doesn't even have a decent picture!" The grainy image within—clearly a screengrab from a surveillance video—showed an indistinct woman who could have been anyone.

Even Agent Whiteclaw was on my side. "This is kind of useless."

"I'm aware it's not much," the boss apologized. "I'm working on getting more info."

"These fires, we're sure it's the chimera causing them? Could be another cryptid with fire."

"It's the chimera," Kowalski confirmed. "Fires are her MO, and we're not going to chalk it up to coincidence when we have a high-risk criminal who just so happens to be around when one of their signature moves is occurring. Besides, I have it on good authority it's her."

"I'll want a copy of the video you mentioned."

"Unfortunately, I can't do that, as it appears to have been misplaced."

"Of course, it was." I held in a sigh. "Very well. Guess I have my work cut out for me."

I'd almost forgotten about Whiteclaw until he murmured, "Don't you mean we?"

I glanced at him. "That will depend on you. My last partner's idea of help was eating and napping while I did all the drudgery."

Whiteclaw's brow arched. "Then I can see why you prefer working alone. If it helps, I never nap and would never dream of eating while watching you work."

If he actually meant that, then maybe this

wouldn't suck balls. "Speaking of eating, I need lunch. How do you feel about tacos? I know a place close by where we can stuff our faces while discussing how to tackle this."

"Lead the way, partner."

I did, sauntering cockily out of my boss's office, happy to be out of the dungeon. As for the extra sway in my step that wiggled my fine ass? Entirely for my new partner's benefit. Sue me. He was damned cute.

CHAPTER 3

Koda did his best to not stare at his new partner's ass. It would have been easier if it weren't so darned perfect. Slap-able. Bite-able. A perfect cushion for pushing.

Not that any of those things would happen. Agent Marissa Smith had made it obvious she didn't like him. Not him specifically, more the fact they'd be working together. Then again, he couldn't entirely blame her. From the sounds of it, her last partner had been an asshole.

He knew all about Ralph, courtesy of Abe Kowalski. He and Abe had met each other long ago while on military missions, and after going civvy, Koda had worked with the man on several government jobs. Only a few days ago Kowalski had contacted him to brief him on the latest gig.

"I put in a request to have you temporarily transferred to my precinct."

"Is this the one you're restructuring because of corrupt management?"

"Yeah. It's still a bit of a mess, but slowly but surely, I'm getting it sorted."

"Just tell me what you need, and I'll be glad to help."

Koda didn't mind. His current CA office in New York had been quiet. Too quiet. Blame the fact he'd helped the city wrangle their local cryptid problem. After all, it was what he did. As a super-agent, he was known as the CA's problem solver. If an office had a tricky situation, they called him in because he knew how to get the job done.

Unusual in this case? The fact Abe wanted him to pair with another agent. Most times, Koda worked his jobs solo. But he could handle whatever challenge got tossed his way, even that of a prickly woman who preferred to work alone.

At least she seemed competent. According to Abe, she stood head and shoulders above the other agents, a claim backed up by her personnel file. Her career and accomplishments proved to be quite impressive. On top of her high success rate when it came to solving crimes, she stood out as one of the few agents not caught up in her precinct's corruption. As a matter of fact, she'd actually helped put a stop to it. More recently, she handled not one but three monsters on her own.

Yes, monsters. While the Cryptid Authority and many others tried to use what they termed non-derogatory language, Koda called it like it was. Beings that caused harm for no reason other than because they enjoyed it were monsters, and this woman knew how to take them down—and look sexy doing it.

The swaying ass exited the precinct and crossed the road to a place titled "Fiesta in Your Mouth." They entered to lightly playing music and the smell of refried beans. Agent Smith didn't look at Koda or the menu as she ordered. "Taco trio, extra hot sauce and cheese."

"And a strawberry lemonade," finished the young woman behind the counter with a smile.

"You know me too well, Bianca. What do you want?" Marissa asked, finally glancing at him over her shoulder.

"I'll have the same," he stated as he pulled out his wallet.

Too slow, as it turned out, seeing as how Marissa had already tapped her phone on the debit machine and paid.

"How much do I owe you?" he asked as he followed her to a table for two by the window.

"Nothing. I buy this time. You get the next."

"Sounds good." At least she assumed there would be a next time. Given the way she'd reacted in Abe's office, he'd expected her to do her best to get rid of him.

"So, Whiteclaw, is it true you're a skinwalker?"

"I am."

"Since you're the first one I've met, I have to ask, do you shift on the full moon only or at will?" A valid question. Many shapeshifters required the moon's rays to morph.

"At will. Now my turn to interrogate. You're a witch." Stated rather than asked. He already knew. All CA agents had some kind of ability. "What element do you specialize in?"

Her lips pursed. "A few. Depending on my goddess's mood."

"Rumor has it you're pretty gifted."

Her shoulders lifted and fell. "I do all right. How much magic I have kind of depends on Hekate's mood. She doesn't always answer when I pray for help."

"Gods can be fickle," he conceded.

Their order was called quickly, and the next few minutes were spent actually enjoying his meal. Flavorful and plenty of, he finished two of his tacos, one beef, one fish, and took a sip of his drink before tackling his third one of chicken. Only once he'd devoured the last bite did he speak again.

"So where do you want to start our investigation?"

"Our?" she repeated with a grimace. "I don't need a partner."

"Neither do I, yet here we are."

Her lips pursed. "Listen, I'm sure the last thing you want to do is be stuck doing some boring research. Feel free to do whatever. If Abe asks, I'll tell him you were a diligent digging mole."

He arched a brow. "How generous, but here's the thing. I enjoy digging. As a matter of fact, I'm known to be a most excellent forager when it comes to information."

She leaned back in her seat and eyed him. "I find that hard to believe."

"Let me guess, because I'm good-looking?" It wasn't just females who had issues being taken seriously where attractiveness was concerned.

"You're not shy, are you?"

"Not one bit. But then again, neither are you."

Her lips quirked. "I never was good at keeping my mouth shut."

"A good thing or the corruption in your precinct would have lasted longer."

At the reminder, she grimaced. "It should have never gone on for that long in the first place. I knew something was amiss; I just lacked the proof."

"It didn't help how many agents, including your previous boss, were caught up in the corruption." He'd been appalled at how deep the rot went. To him, the Cryptid Authority stood for justice.

"I see you read up on us."

"I told you I like to dig. Now, on to the job at hand."

"How much did Abe brief you on the chimera situation?"

"I know they think she's setting fires and the sightings of her suggest that she's heading in this direction. That they want us to look at local fires to see if we can make a connection."

"I wish the file on her wasn't so useless." Her lips twisted. "Why even bother handing it over, given everything is redacted? We have basically nothing to go on, and his only suggestion is to investigate arson cases to rule out the chimera's involvement."

"Which is a waste of time."

Her eyes widened in surprise. "Agreed."

"Personally, I think we should be looking into the fires where she was confirmed involved and see if we can spot a pattern."

"That's actually not a bad idea," she murmured. "I just can't believe that video footage was *lost*." She offered finger air quotes.

"Lost my ass," he stated, once more managing to surprise her judging by her expression. "The redacted file makes it kind of obvious someone is trying to cover for the chimera."

"If that were the case, why even have us investigate?"

"Because, while there might be some trying to hide her actions, Abe isn't one to turn a blind eye."

"Why, Whiteclaw, are you implying there's rot in the higher-up CA ranks?"

"I'd say it's obvious and expected given an organization of our size."

She leaned back with her drink, her full lips wrapped around the straw as she gave it a long suck. He shifted in his seat to divert his mind. which seemed determined to go down a dirty path.

"Why would anyone want a chimera, or any cryptid for that matter, to cause trouble with humans? The fact remains humans outnumber nonhumans and, if they so choose, could easily turn on the nons."

"But would they win?" he countered. "I don't know if you're aware, but there is a faction that isn't happy with the rules imposed on cryptids."

"What rules?" she scoffed. "Cryptids live as free as humans."

"But are required to be registered."

"Which isn't a big deal."

"To you, but there are some that chafe. Who find it degrading. Who don't like the fact they have to keep their gifts harnessed. There are even some who question the rule of 'do no harm to humans.' I know the vampires have been grumbling about the fact they have to drink from a donated bag and can no longer suck from the source unless they are legally entered into a binding agreement with a human."

"You make it sound like there's a massive cooperative conspiracy by some of the more violent cryptids to start a war with humanity."

"Because I think there is."

She stared at him before slowly saying, "I'm surprised you're telling me this. How do you know I'm not part of this conspiracy?"

"I've read your file. You're upright as they come."

"My boss would disagree."

"Your boss says you're the best agent he has." As she preened at the compliment, he tempered it with, "But he worries about the fact that you don't play nice and tend to rush in without a care for your safety. He's convinced it will get you killed."

The statement brought a scowl. "I'm not going to sit on my hands while bad shit happens."

"Agreed. Hence why he asked me to partner with you. Together, we're going to get to the bottom of this chimera mystery. And if it happens to uncover some uncomfortable truths..."

"Then so be it." She smiled, a genuine one that lit up her whole face. As people came in and sat at the table behind them, they gave each other knowing looks. Time to change the subject to something more innocuous in case they listened. "Where are you from?"

"New York."

"You're far from home."

"Not really. I moved away a long time ago, and currently, I don't have roots anywhere. I tend to live as a nomad, going where I'm needed."

"You don't get lonely?"

"Nah. What about you? Where are you from?"

"Here. I've lived in the area since I graduated and was assigned to this precinct."

"Not interested in exploring the world?"

She shrugged. "Never really thought about it, to be honest."

"Guess the fact you have roots and family gives you a good reason to stay."

At that claim, she shook her head. "Nope. Nobody

in town to hold me back unless my houseplants count."

The people behind them rose and left when their order was called, leaving Koda and Marissa in privacy once more.

She drummed her fingers on the table and returned to business. "Your plan to study the previous suspected incidents is a good one. Guess we should hit the bullpen to see if we can snag a computer and start poking."

He grimaced. "Do we have to? I'm not much of an office guy."

"I don't invite strange men to my place." Her quick reply.

His lips quirked. "Wouldn't dream of it. I was thinking more like a park or something. Fresh air helps me think. I can hotspot my laptop if we need to do any online research."

For a second, he thought she'd refuse, but she nodded her head. "I know a spot we can go. I'll drive."

And by drive, she meant somewhat psychotically, if adeptly. She maneuvered through traffic as if she played *Mario Kart*, taking them just outside of town to a wooded area. The sign just before the small parking lot named it *Penelope's Conversation Area*.

He emerged from the car to ask, "Who's Penelope?"

"Legend has it she was a witch who long ago saved the townspeople from a devastating forest fire but lost her life in the process. The woods were dedicated in her name."

"Nice story."

"It is on the surface until you dig deeper and realize she was actually a sorceress who planned to open a portal to Hell, only to have her spell backfire and consume her."

"And no one has exposed the truth to get her cancelled and rename the park?"

"Oh, they know. They just choose to ignore it because her actions actually led to the town prospering, as the fire ended up exposing a vein of gold that they've been using to keep taxes low but residential services high."

He snorted. "So a good thing out of the bad situation."

"Exactly." She plopped the folder Abe gave her onto a picnic table before perching her ass on the wooden top, her feet planted on the bench. "How shall we do this?"

"Abe says you've got a fine eye for detail. How about you start reading the details of the fires and toss tidbits at me, which I can dig deeper into?"

"Do you always flatter your partners outrageously?"

"No." He didn't mention he usually worked alone. "But Abe doesn't give praise lightly. So let's see if his claims of your being smart are true."

Laughter burst out of her, a low husky chuckle that tightened his groin. "I don't know about smart. You never met my last partner. Anyone compared to him would come off as a genius."

"Guess we'll see then. I'll start by seeing what the internet has to publicly say about the chimera we're searching for."

"If it's a chimera."

He pursed his lips. "You think it might be something else?"

"I'm saying we should keep an open mind and see where the evidence leads." She thumbed through the folder with a frown. "Abe stated she'd been locked up for crimes against humanity, and that fires were her MO, but"—she poked a finger at a large, redacted section—"why would they have blocked out details of her crimes in her official file?"

"I find it even odder we don't have a name. You'd think they would have her legal appellation in here somewhere, but she's only referred to as the chimera. Shouldn't a known prisoner have something other than her breed to call her by?"

"I hadn't even noticed that, I'd just jumped to the meat of the case." Agent Smith pursed her lips. "Very odd."

And it got weirder. A search didn't bring up anything that could be attributed to this chimera. At least nothing in North America in the last few decades. The only stories he found revolved around Europe and the Middle East. Even the recent fire at the cell phone shop was labelled suspected arson and not cryptid. Very strange, to say the least, considering online conspiracy influencers loved to report on potential cryptid crimes.

He glanced at Marissa, who held up a sheet to the sun as if she could read through the blacked-out sections.

"Does that actually work?" he asked.

"No. This is ridiculous," she snapped, slapping down the paper. "Even the most recent fire being attributed to her has the bare minimum of details. The B and E and arson report doesn't even mention the word chimera, just possible cryptid activity suspected."

"I am not finding a thing online either."

"If I didn't know better, I'd believe you were right about someone intentionally scrubbing information about the chimera—not just the CA file, but also public-facing records."

"This is too thorough to be a coincidence."

Agent Smith played devil's advocate. "Is it, though? I mean, her original crimes would have been more than thirty years ago, when the internet was in the baby stages and the news media didn't have a big foothold. Add in the fact that once she went to prison there would have been nothing to report."

"But we do have recent news, and I'm not just talking about the fire. She's not listed anywhere as one of the escapees when the prison was destroyed."

"Really?" Her eyebrows rose. "Yet Kowalski claims she was one of the escapees. So what does he and the agency know that we don't?" She rose from the picnic table to pace around the area.

Koda snapped his fingers. "The lost video... Someone had to have watched it and known it showed a suspect, otherwise why turn it in to the cops? Is there a name of the owner of that video on any of the reports?"

"Good question. Let me see." She leaned over the folder, and he quickly averted his gaze, as the neckline of her shirt gaped enough for him to see the upper swell of her breasts. Not quick enough to avoid a bit of action below the belt.

Blame his lack of dating. It had been years since his last relationship. In his defense, he moved around a lot, and he didn't often meet women that piqued his interest. Agent Smith, though... She definitely intrigued. Sharp, beautiful, and not one of those giggly star-struck sycophants he usually encountered when he dropped into a new precinct.

She lifted a sheet and waved it. "The police report doesn't have a witness name. Just says video evidence from the adult store across the street showed a female exiting the electronic store before the fire started."

"Meaning those taking statements were either incredibly incompetent or purposely vague."

"Most likely the former. Initially, human cops were the ones investigating. Then they handed it over to the CA."

"And the CA didn't follow up."

"Um, what do you think we're doing?"

"Not our assigned task, which was investigating fires in this town to see if we can connect them to the chimera." He eyed her as his mind whirled. "Still don't think there's a cover-up happening?"

"Oh, I think there is, but I'm the kind of person who likes hard evidence before making accusations."

"Then let's get that evidence. Want to road trip?"

The abrupt question didn't throw her off balance, as she immediately asked, "To where?"

"Well, I don't know about you, but I'm not one to call witnesses and try to get them to spill their guts on the phone."

Her lips curved. "You want to talk to the sex shop employee who handed over the footage."

"I do. So, what do you say? Shall we take a drive?"

"It's a three-hour trip, and we're already midafternoon," Marissa pointed out.

"Would you prefer to go in the morning?"

She scuffed the ground with her feet before shaking her head. "No. Let's do it. Our chances are better of catching the person who was on duty that night if we arrive later in the day. Not to mention, we have no other leads currently."

"Do you need to grab anything before we go?"

"Nope. You?"

He shook his head, although he did wish he'd brought a spare pair of pants, given Marissa drove, and what should have taken three hours was done in just over two.

CHAPTER 4

THE DRIVE WENT BY QUICKLY AND NOT JUST BECAUSE I SPED A tad bit over the limit. My new partner actually kept digging for info while en route, his laptop balanced on his knees.

Even better, he wasn't afraid to search outside the box.

"I might have found something," he muttered, an hour into our trip.

"Anything would be better than the zilch we have so far." My reply.

"So while the regular internet doesn't have any deets on the chimera, turns out the dark web does make a few mentions."

"Wait, you know how to access the dark web?" To be fair, I'd never tried. I had this belief that the moment I did, I'd be outed as a narc.

"I've got ins with a few places; fairy court, dwarven caverns, even a contact under the sea."

"Impressive."

"Useful."

"So what did you find?"

"Our chimera has a bounty on her head."

"Well duh. She's an escaped criminal. Most likely the family of someone she killed would like to see her wiped off the face of the Earth."

"They don't want her dead. The bounty is for ten million if captured alive."

I'll admit I swerved. "Ten mil?" I whistled. "That is a lot of dough. Wonder why they're willing to pay so much."

"I can think of a few reasons. Personal zoo. Hunter safari. Experimentation. Revenge."

My mouth rounded. "All but the last are kind of depraved."

"But happen," his grim reply. "I have to wonder if perhaps the person offering the bounty is also the one wiping all traces of the chimera."

"Wouldn't that make it more difficult for anyone to find the chimera and claim the prize?"

"It would. Another theory is someone is trying to hide her so that the bounty hunters can't locate her."

"That seems a little convoluted."

"Just spit-balling," he replied.

My fingers danced on the steering wheel as I thought. "Is there a way to find out who's placed the bounty?"

"It's the dark web. Anonymity is the norm."

"Okay, but whoever is offering it surely has a way

to be contacted when someone does finally capture the chimera."

"Contact, yes, but again, anonymous. Arrangements would have to be made to do a transfer."

"They might have info that could prove useful to us."

"They won't talk to CA agents. People on the dark web often don't want to expose themselves—or their secrets—to any kind of law enforcement."

"So we'd have to offer some kind of tit-for-tat to make it worth their while," I mused.

"The bounty thing is really bugging you," he added.

"I've got a feeling it's important." I just couldn't have articulated why, but I'd learned to trust my gut. It rarely led me astray.

We finished the drive without any more big revelations and pulled up to the sex shop just before dinner. It certainly didn't attempt to be discreet with its flashing neon sign titled *Boobs and Butts Galore*. I especially cringed that the double O in boobs were actually breasts with tassel-covered nipples.

Agent Whiteclaw stood beside me, a towering presence that stirred up all kids of steamy feelings that, surprisingly, I didn't want to smother. Yet.

Instead of walking toward the sex shop, I turned to look at the site of the arson. I'd already known there wasn't much left of the structure as I'd seen pictures of it in the file. Without solid structures, I'd be limited on how much information I might be able to glean from it.

Even so, I started walking towards it.

"Where are you going?"

"To check out the fire scene," I said, hurrying across the street, which was void of traffic at this hour of the night.

"I don't know what you expect to find," he said, catching up to me. "The CA went over it already."

"You don't work with witches very often, do you Agent Whiteclaw?" I gave him a teasing smile that I wasn't sure he could see, considering we stood in the dark. The fire had even taken out the parking lot lights. To remedy that, I created a light orb that bobbed in front of me.

Without waiting for him to answer, I walked the perimeter of the store's remains, touching each post that had stayed standing.

"Mind telling me what you're hoping to find?"

"Memories," I told him. "Unfortunately, I'm not getting anything, since almost everything is gone. The more of a structure there is—four walls, a floor, a ceiling—the more is available to hold imprints. But here... I got nothing." Not even an imprint of chimera essence. I still envied those other CA witches with that ability.

He waited for me to finish without asking any more questions. Defeated, I finally gave up and returned to our car in the sex shop parking lot, my stoic partner following.

"You okay going inside?" he asked when I hesitated.

Why would I have a problem going inside a store full of sex toys and lingerie with the hottest dude I'd spent time with in ages? Guess I'd soon see exactly what kind of guy I'd been partnered with. Would he be the sort of man who turned this into an opportunity for sexual innuendo or would Agent Whiteclaw remain a professional?

"Why would I have an issue? Sex is a natural bodily function."

"It is." He uttered deadpan.

"Shall we get this over with?" I demanded with more gusto than I felt.

While not a prude by any means, there was something about walking into a sex shop alongside a hunk that made my cheeks heat, especially since I had no idea where to look. Should I stare at the wall of dildos? The racks of bondage wear and lingerie? What about the triple X movie wall with its poster of *I Want You Stretching My Ass*, part seventeen?

I chose to focus on the register at the counter, behind which sat a guy with blond dreadlocks and a scraggly beard. The clerk, attention locked on his phone, didn't look over at us despite the bell announcing our presence.

My partner didn't seem perturbed at all by our environ and strode straight for the fellow. "Afternoon, sir. Could I have a moment of your time?"

"Sure." The guy put his phone to the side. "What

can I help you with? Looking for something to spice up the bedroom with your lady?" His gaze slid to me, and I had to retort.

"We're not here for your merchandise but to ask questions." I then flashed my badge. "Cryptid Authority, here on official business."

Some people got freaked out when they heard who I worked for. Not this guy. His eyes brightened, and his posture straightened. "You're here about the fire."

"We are. Were you the one who handed over the video footage to the police?"

"Yup. And I saw it happening."

"Wait, you actually witnessed it?" I couldn't help my surprise. The fact there'd been an eyewitness wasn't mentioned in the report.

"Yeah. Good thing, too, since the cops lost the recording I gave them. How do you accidentally misplace evidence?" The clerk shook his head in disbelief.

I totally understood.

"You don't have a backup of your surveillance?" my partner asked.

"Nah. Video files take up a huge amount of data storage, so the camera just deletes anything older than a few days to save new stuff. The few times we've had issues with shoplifters and the 'you're-all-going-to-hell' folks, the cops come in with a hard drive, save the footage, and handle it all from there."

"Can you tell us what you saw that night?" I pulled

out a pad of paper and pen more for show than note-taking.

"Sure. So it was late. Like almost midnight, and I'd just finished checking out this *fine* woman"—he gestured to the register—"and was treating myself to a look as she walked away. She had one hell of an ass, let me tell you—"

"Get on with it," Koda growled.

"Right, well I was watching her leave when I seen the woman coming out the cell phone store across the street."

"Do you have a description?" Whiteclaw interrupted.

"Not really. She had a hood on."

My turn to interject with, "Then what makes you call them a woman?"

"Because she had curves like this." The clerk mimed an hourglass figure.

"Did they have a limp or a strange way of walking?" my partner questioned.

"Nah. Looked one hundred percent normal if you ignored the fact that the place had closed hours before but she left with a store bag in one hand."

Which most likely contained a cell phone, given the store's business.

"You didn't see her going in?" I backtracked for more info.

"Not in person, no. But the tape I gave the cops caught her. She walked right up to the door and paused for a second with her hand on it before going inside."

I assumed the pause would be when she used magic to disable alarms and unlock the door. I nodded and made a note of it. "How long after she left did the fire start?"

"About twenty minutes."

"That long?" Another detail missing in the report. I glanced at Whiteclaw. Did he also wonder why it took so long before the flames really got going? Had she done something to delay the fire?

My partner had a different query for the clerk. "When did you call in the crime?"

"You mean the fire? Once I saw the flames. I didn't call in a B and E because, honestly, I didn't think much of the woman I saw. I mean, I thought maybe she was staff, leaving after a restock shift."

"A staff member using the front entrance instead of the back?"

He shrugged. "Sometimes ladies prefer the more well-lit exits and she didn't seem like a thief. No alarms were going off or nothing."

"Any other tidbits you can recall about the woman?" Whiteclaw pushed. "Approximate height? Maybe something distinguishing?"

The clerk rolled his shoulders. "Not really. Like I said, she wore a hood so her face was hidden and a long coat cinched at the waist."

Too vague to be helpful.

"How do you feel about magic?" I queried.

Knowing the resistance I sometimes encountered from non-cryptids, I found it wise to lead with questioning before suggesting a magical visual recap.

"Depends on the kind. I got some magic-infused dildos that my girlfriend swears by over the battery-operated ones." More info than I needed to know, but it at least told me that he wasn't abhorrent to my craft.

"Would you be okay with showing me what you remember from that night?"

"How?" He finally didn't look so relaxed as he frowned.

"It won't hurt," I hastened to reassure. "I just need to hold your hand and have you think about what you witnessed, and I'll be able to project an image of it for my partner and me to watch."

"You're going to mind-read me?" His eyes widened, and I wanted to curse. People tended to get wiggy about the thought of people prodding inside their heads.

"Not exactly. It's more making visual what you'll be thinking loudly. I can't actually poke inside you for secrets or make you do things." A lie. Technically I could, but I wouldn't. That kind of dark magic could have serious side effects, like turning a person's brain into mush.

"Oh, I don't mind if you see my secrets, but you should know they're mostly dirty." He leered, and I did my best to not cringe.

"Ready?" I asked, holding out my hand.

"Fuck yeah." He immediately put his dry fingers against mine.

"Think of that night. What you saw," I murmured softly as I pushed out some magic, shaping the intent of the spell that it might grab his surface thoughts.

The storefront window and the glimpse out of it appeared as an image midair, but it then jumped around to various quick-flashing glimpses of strange things, like a breakfast sandwich then the face of a woman with pouty lips. The guy huffed, "Cool."

"Focus," I chided. "Show us what you saw."

I ignored the main focus of the memory—the backside of the female customer in a white crop top and black leggings—and focused on the mobile phone store. The streetlights illuminated enough to see across the road to the store that in present-times stood as a charred husk.

The door to the other business opened, and the clerk's memory shifted toward the figure that exited. They wore, as previously described, a flowing trench coat made of a dark material belted at the waist, with a deep hood that hid facial features. I could see why the clerk called the figure a woman given their hourglass shape, but that didn't mean much these days. The supposed burglar-arsonist didn't pause or hesitate but strode off briskly, bag swinging from their hand.

"That's it," the clerk stated. The random thoughts in his mind once more began to seep; flashing lights from a fire truck then the cops who came to question him.

It led to me guiding him to another memory. "Show me what you remember of the fire." Probably not useful, but years of investigating meant I knew every tidbit helped.

The clerk's memory of it started when the window blew out across the street. One moment he stared at his phone—with images of big-titted women—then he heard an explosion. He whipped his head around to look out the window and he saw smoke and fire billowing from the store across the street. The flames undulated and stretched outward into the night, violet-hued, not red or orange, making them magic and not propellant-based. A detail also not in the report, but not too surprising seeing as the file had damn near nothing in it anyway.

I would have let the clerk go at that point, but my new partner had one more request. "What do you remember of the video you gave the cops? Specifically the part where it showed the woman going in?"

The clerk's slack expression showed him shifting thoughts, the next recollection showing the screen of a monitor as he scrolled back through video footage, too far, then skipped forward, stopping as the suspect walked into frame. They paused with their hand on the door and glanced over their shoulder, just for a second, then quickly entered the mobile phone store. They weren't inside for long before emerging with the bag. The memory then revealed the clerk jumping the video forward, stopping twenty-three minutes later when the window exploded and the fire began, confirming his story.

"That was great. Thank you," I murmured. I went to pull my hand free, but before I did, the clerk's memory changed to something that had never happened.

Me, wearing something widely revealing, my lips full and pouting as I kneeled and looked up seductively.

Oh gross.

I quickly broke contact before I could see what the clerk would visualize next. The guy didn't even have the decency to look abashed by his lewd thoughts. He grinned.

I stayed focused on business, least I give in to my urge to punch him. "The customer who was leaving your place as the suspect was leaving the mobile store, do you have any info on her?" She could have a better description of the other woman, considering she'd been right across from her.

The clerk gave his head a shake. "Nope. We don't collect customer info. And before you ask, she paid with cash. No credit card to trace. We can go back in my memory if you want to see what she looks like from the front, but that'll only be helpful if you're good at identifying people by tits." He laughed, and the itch to slug him grew stronger.

"That's alright, we're good," Koda answered while I seethed. "Thank you for your cooperation."

"If you need anything, and I mean *anything*, I'm here until two."

I practically raced out of the store, Whiteclaw on my heels.

As we emerged onto the sidewalk, I heaved out a breath. "I need to wash my hand."

My partner snorted. "I don't blame you. That guy was slimy and, on top of it, didn't even give us a good lead." He reached into his pocket and pulled out a small bottle of hand sanitizer, squeezing some into my hand when I reached my palm out.

"Thanks." I rubbed the liquid into my hands, grateful for it, though still feeling it wasn't enough to cleanse myself of the clerk's taint. "But I wouldn't say we didn't get a lead. It was a good call asking him to remember the early part of the video." I unlocked my car door and slid into the driver's side.

Whiteclaw seated himself on the passenger side before asking, "How was it good? It didn't really give us anything we didn't know."

"Wrong." I twisted my hand and reproduced that last vision, only I paused it at the moment the suspect turned their head to look over their shoulder. I then zoomed in on the hood, which had the right angle to show me most of a face. A woman's face, the ageless kind that showed maturity but no wrinkles. Lips thin but shapely, nose straight and narrow. Her eyes remained partially shadowed, but one definitely glinted ice-chip blue, and a hank of long hair peeked, the same electric blue.

My partner whistled. "We have a description. Nice job."

The praise warmed until sobering reality set in. "I'm not sure what to do with this information since we're both in agreement that there seems to be a cover-up."

"What do you mean?"

"I mean, normally I'd update my boss on the mission progress."

"Abe's not part of a cover-up," Koda quickly said. "He's a good guy. I've known him a long time."

"Yeah, but he assigned us to look at local fires, not go back and poke at this one. He might not be involved in a cover-up, but that doesn't mean he'd be pleased we went off-task."

"Right. So we keep all this between the two of us. Tell no one else. For now."

"Agreed."

I couldn't help a nagging sense of unease as we drove back.

With good reason, as it turned out. When I hit the precinct the next morning, it was to find a grim-faced Whiteclaw.

"What's up?" I asked.

He handed me his phone. The screen showed a bold headline.

Sex Shop Owner Killed in Overnight Robbery.

The eyewitness had been eliminated.

CHAPTER 5

Koda wondered what Agent Smith thought as she read the article about the sex shop clerk's death. She showed nothing of her emotions, and yet she had to be freaking. He knew he was. Whoever covered the chimera's tracks appeared willing to kill... and they seemed to be keeping an eye on his and Smith's movements.

"Could be the chimera had been sticking around, admiring her handiwork." He offered the most logical suggestion. "Saw agents go in and talk to the clerk and only then realized she had left a loose end."

Agent Smith shook her head slightly, seeming as unconvinced as he felt. Her voice emerged flat as she said, "I'm grabbing a coffee from across the street. Want one?"

"Sure."

They didn't speak as they exited the precinct. She waited until they were midway across the road before murmuring, "If the chimera had stuck around after she burned down the phone store, then she would have already seen the witness talking to the cops and taken him out sooner. I'd bet anything it wasn't her. Who knows we went to see the clerk?"

"I didn't tell anyone."

"Not even Abe?"

"Nope."

"Me either, but we also didn't hide our presence. Anyone could have seen us go in, not to mention the store cameras would have a record of us. The interior ones probably even caught me casting that spell on him for his memories."

A few choice words emerged in a mutter before he growled, "You heard the guy yesterday. He's no stranger to robberies."

"Please," his partner drawled as she pulled on the coffee shop door. "You don't really believe it's a coincidence, do you?"

No, he didn't.

They ordered their coffees, but rather than drink them at the tiny, cramped tables, they returned to the sidewalk.

She took a sip before speaking. "I wish we could go there and I could pull a memory from the store, but the article said he was shot as he exited the shop."

"And your powers can't replay a past event from outside."

"Open air has no way of holding memories." She shook her head sadly. "So now what? If we rule out that this was the chimera's handiwork, and we table the idea that this was an armed robbery, then what are we looking at?"

"Someone trying to cover the chimera's tracks. Someone who thought they did that when they 'lost' the original video and ensured any mention of the witness was left out of the file."

"And if the person wiping the chimera's existence is willing to kill, we might have made ourselves a target. After all, we've now seen with our own eyes the same thing that clerk did. Not to mention, we're actively seeking her."

"I'll talk to Abe about putting you in protective custody."

"Oh hell no." She shook her head. "You're not locking me away like some damsel in distress."

"But you're the one who just pointed out the danger."

"I'm a Cryptid Authority agent. Danger is part of the job. I am not going to let whoever is manipulating events get away with this. It just makes me more determined to catch them."

"Very well." He respected the fact she wouldn't back down. "Guess we need to plan our next move."

"We don't have many. We don't know why the chimera wanted a phone bad enough to come out of hiding after all this time."

"To call someone." He said it deadpan, and she snorted.

"Ha. Smartass. Still doesn't help us know why

someone is wiping evidence. Just like we don't know who or why someone put a bounty on her."

"Could be the bounty is encouraging hunters to hide evidence of the chimera's movement so other hunters are thrown off and they can claim the reward for themselves."

"That wouldn't account for why our official files lack information, or why so much is redacted."

"That's assuming there's only one cover-up person. Could be one person in the CA did the inside cover-up and someone unrelated is wiping the internet, stealing videos, and killing witnesses. We have no idea how many could be involved."

"I don't know." She tapped on the lid of her cup thoughtfully. "I don't think a bounty hunter is going to take that much time and put that much effort into covering their target's track. It would put them way behind if they hung around one spot when their target is on the move."

"I think you're right. We can probably rule out bounty hunters."

She nodded, then looked off into the distance, her jaw set firm as her mind worked. He couldn't help but admire her beauty as the wind picked up strands of her bright pink hair. Despite the unconventional color, Marissa looked the picture of an ideal agent. Smart, determined, capable. All attractive traits—which he really shouldn't be thinking so much about.

"Right now I'm racking my brain as to where we

should poke around next." Her words knocked him out of his thoughts.

"How about the other three fires being attributed to her?"

"What's there to look at?" She shook her head in frustration. "At least we had a video to go off of for the last one. The first three have no videos, no witnesses. I can't run a memory spell to replay the structures' last moments since they're nothing but ash, like the phone store."

"All we have to go off of is some CA agents' determination that those fires were caused by the chimera.

"And quite frankly, I'm not convinced they were."

Koda blinked at her in surprise. "Why do I get the impression you know something I don't?"

"More like a niggling feeling that we're missing something." She stood abruptly. "We need to hit the library."

The oddness of her statement had him frowning. "What on earth for?"

"Research."

"Wouldn't it be easier to do that on a computer at the precinct?"

"It would, but I'm going to assume any search we do will be noted. Possibly passed on to the wrong person."

"The corruption in your CA office should have been wiped out."

"Assuming everyone was caught. And let's say they

were. Nothing to say an outsider doesn't have spyware keeping an eye."

The suggestion turned him pensive. "Meaning we can't trust even our phones or laptops."

"Now you get it."

"It could explain how even though we told no one where we went yesterday, we might have been tracked."

"Also correct." She held up her phone and made a show of cracking it open and pulling the battery. She tucked both cell and the battery in her oversized purse. "Now no one can follow me."

He mimicked her actions but noted, "Unless they've placed a tracking hex on us."

Her lips quirked. "As if I wouldn't notice. I scanned you as we exited the precinct. You're clean, and I've got a shield against magical interference."

"Good thinking."

"I'm not just good looks," she retorted.

While she might be super attractive, he did agree. She had a very sharp mind, could problem solve, and, even better, came up with solutions.

"Where is this library?" he asked.

"Not far, but we'll have to take a bit of a detouring path in case someone is following."

"Pretty sure I'd notice a tail."

"I'm not worried about the two-legged kind," she replied as she began walking.

"Are you always this suspicious?" He kept pace with her easily.

"Aren't you?"

"Depends on the situation."

She turned into an alley, her pace rapid, and as they passed the midway point, she waved a hand over her shoulder. A quick glance behind showed a shimmer across the narrow space, and for a second, a section of it trembled as if something had run into it.

They emerged onto the next street, and she skipped across the road right into another alley. Which led to another wave of her fingers. This time he didn't see any shimmering.

They did this several times before she ducked into an old church, the stone of it dark with grime that came from age. The inside offered up a dry musty smell. The carpet on the floor appeared worn bare in spots. A bulletin board held fliers, some printed, others handwritten. Bible study. AA group meeting times. Jesus loves you.

A part of him wanted to ask why they needed to go inside the church, but instead, he continued to follow. All would surely become clear.

His partner led him into the church proper with its wooden pews and worn red runner carpet going up the aisle. An altar with a white draping cloth sat under a suspended cross with a Jesus nailed to it, the head bowed with its crown of thorns, the body gaunt.

Having been raised on a reserve, he'd never understood the allure of a religion with one god, and a seemingly cruel one at that. He'd been taught of the primal gods, the ones of rain and sun, moon and the hunt.

The door tucked beside the organ proved to be her destination, and she slipped through it into a tiny chamber lined with hooks that held white robes. In a corner leaned several tall candlesticks.

He glanced around, seeing no exit, not even a window. "I think this is a dead end."

"Not quite." Agent Smith knelt on the floor and touched the planks. While he didn't see her do anything, she must have triggered some kind of mechanism because, with a soft click, a section of the wooden floor shifted sideways exposing a hole with stairs descending into darkness.

Without hesitation, his partner headed down.

He followed more cautiously. He almost flinched when the trap door slid shut, sealing them in the hidden basement—and the dark.

While unmanly, he did feel some relief when a ball of light appeared, meaning he could see Agent Smith and the passageway they found themselves in. The tightly mortared brick and stone formed a tunnel and appeared quite old but solid.

"Dare I ask how you knew about this secret place?" he asked.

"A few years ago, the church had a problem with their wine and wafers being stolen. They tried everything to stop it. Replaced locks on the outside doors. Installed cameras outside. They even hired a few security guards, but they all quit, claiming the church was haunted. The human pastor contacted the CA when he ran out of options. It took only one night on stakeout to realize it wasn't ghosts but goblins that were sneaking in, using this secret tunnel system to cause mischief."

"You arrested them?"

"No. They weren't being malicious. Just hungry and thirsty. The dumpster they used to feed out of stopped having food because a restaurant went out of business. I found them a new home with plenty of stuff to keep them satisfied."

"That was kind of you."

She rolled her shoulders. "I guess. To me, it seemed better than wasting time and resources convicting them of petty theft and putting them in containment." The centers being for the nonviolent cryptids that couldn't obey the rules of society.

"Where does this passageway lead?"

She walked slightly ahead of him, her ball of light bobbing. "A few places. This underground network was built a long time ago and links to some of the founding edifices such as the Griffon Hotel, the now-closed-down opera house, the original fire station before the town got too big, and the library."

"How many people know about them?"

She shook her head. "None that I'm aware of. I avoided mentioning it in my report once I fixed the problem."

"Why?"

Her glance over the shoulder showed a mischievous smile. "Never know when a girl might need to go skulking around town without notice."

They walked for several minutes and passed two intersections before she halted at a dead end. This time, he knew better than to question and waited while she pressed her hand against the stone with a tiny inscribed circle. Magic tingled his skin as the solid wall shifted to form stairs leading upward to a ceiling that suddenly had a gaping opening.

They emerged into a musty chamber filled with three rows of bookcases, the shelves packed tight with books. Sconces glowed, giving the space a warm vibe at odds with the ugly gargoyle statues perched atop the bookcases. The walls were the same stone as the tunnel, the floor as well. Only the shelves were made of wood.

He glanced around and noticed not only was there no other exit but cobwebs decorated corners and dust left silt on the floor and shelves. "I don't get the impression this library is used much."

"Because it hasn't been for at least a century. From what I've gleaned, whoever used to maintain this library was most likely killed during the cryptid purge in the early nineteen hundreds. It led to the texts hidden in this secret chamber being lost."

"Until you found them." He shook his head in wonder. "You are a woman full of surprises. And this is an incredible find. I'm surprised it's remained untouched."

"Before you give me shit for keeping this secret, I knew the books in here would be confiscated and tucked away where no one could ever see them. I'm a person who doesn't believe in hiding away knowledge."

"So am I. You needn't worry I'll tell. I'm familiar with authorities concealing uncomfortable truths and histories." It was a harsh fact written in the history of his people, so he appreciated someone who understood sometimes certain rules had to be skirted. He'd seen history being rewritten to hide inconvenient historical facts. It would be a shame for this veritable treasure trove to disappear.

As she began to wander the aisles, her fingers trailing on spines, he wondered aloud, "What are we looking for?"

Agent Smith glanced at him. "The clerk's recollection of the fire has been bothering me."

"You said the timing seemed off."

"Because it was. I mean, yes, it's possible the fire might have taken twenty minutes to get fully going, but I'm not sure a chimera started it."

Her claim gave him pause. "Who could it be then? The video footage didn't show anyone else exiting."

"Not from the front."

"You think it was the person that keeps wiping her tracks?"

"Maybe. Something about the flames is bothering me. Do you recall the color?"

"Purple-ish, meaning magic-induced."

"Magic, yes, but for some reason, my brain keeps insisting it's not the right color for a chimera's fire.

Hence why we're here. I want to see if there's any information about a chimera's abilities."

"And you didn't want to do a search on the internet in case you're being watched."

"Yup." She paused before a book and pulled it out, the dust on it hanging lazily in the air before slowly dropping.

"Did you find something?" He neared enough to see the tight handwritten script on the yellowed pages.

"A book on fire-based cryptids." She slapped it shut and put it back.

"So? What's the verdict?"

Her head shook. "The index showed nothing on chimeras. It only mentioned the North American cryptids that have fire. Chimera are Greek-based, meaning we need something European or even Middle Eastern, seeing as how the manticore is considered to be a close relative. We should split up to look."

They spent the next hour checking out the titles on spines, pulling promising books out, looking for references. The amount of knowledge in this small room staggered. He would love to return to study a few when they solved this case.

Agent Smith joined him at one point, lips down, shoulders rounded. "This is impossible. I know there's got to be something in here, but some of the books are so old I can't read their titles or they're in a language I don't understand."

"Crazy idea, how about a spell to locate what we need?"

She blinked at him. "Why didn't I think of that?"

"Because usually, in a normal library, we'd be able to do a search on a computer and be told exactly where to find a book."

"Never thought I'd miss the old days of the Dewey Decimal System." She laughed, her cheek dimpling on one side, her eyes bright with amusement.

Beautiful. A good thing she turned away or she might have noticed his admiration.

She murmured to herself, "A spell of scrying to find a specific book. It needs a parameter, though, like a fixed image that might match a drawing." She closed her eyes and held out her hands. A faint glow surrounded her.

Her brow furrowed, and the air grew staticky. It sizzled his exposed skin and lifted the ends of his hair.

The books on the shelves began to vibrate, shook hard enough he heard thumps as books fell to the floor.

As quickly as it started, the strangeness ceased. The air returned to normal. The tomes stopped shaking.

His partner opened her eyes and said, "Did anything pop out?"

He strode to the two books lying on the floor, mere paces apart. One was labelled *The Life and Times of a Nymph*. The other had no title, though. As Agent Smith neared, he handed them to her. "I'll check to see if any others wiggled out in the other rows."

There didn't appear to be anything else of interest except for a single sheet of paper partially stuck under a bookcase that he didn't recall from before. As he stooped to grab it, he heard his partner exclaim, "We have company."

CHAPTER 6

The spell drained me more than I liked. A scrying spell shouldn't have been so hard to cast, but it was clear something about the setting had made my work more taxing than usual. Perhaps the room had a built-in resistance to magic to avoid accidental detection and maybe even to protect the treasure trove of knowledge within. In any case, scrying in there took an unseemly amount of magic, and now I found myself weak, hence happy when Agent Whiteclaw offered to look for more books.

Despite my exhaustion, I eyed with interest the pair of books that had popped out. The nymph one seemed more like a biography, but just in case, I tucked it into my purse. The nameless one had me intrigued, especially since I opened it to see unfamiliar script.

Before I could even think of asking Hekate for help deciphering, a scraping noise had me glancing behind.

The hidden hatch, which had closed upon our entry, now gaped wide open. While nothing emerged, I knew it hadn't been triggered by happenstance.

Friend. Foe. Didn't matter. "We have company," I announced to warn my partner, not worried about being heard. If someone did lie in wait, they already knew of our presence.

I tucked the book I held into my purse and shoved the bag so it hung at my backside. I approached the hole with the stairs, hands out, alert and ready for anything. I now kind of wished I'd not depleted a good chunk of my reservoir casting the scrying.

Nothing popped up from the hatch. I stood right over it and glanced down. Nothing appeared to be waiting below.

Agent Whiteclaw barked, "On the ceiling."

What? I'd only just tilted my head upward when something dropped from above. Solidly built, the stone body heavy, the gargoyle took me to the floor hard.

And, yes, I meant actual gargoyle. Most likely a guardian of the library activated when I used my magic. In all my previous visits, the statues sat inert atop the bookcases, and I'd never paid them any mind, making the assumption—wrongly—that they were the decorative, and not the real, variety.

As the gargoyle opened its mouth, showing off jagged stone teeth, I wondered how to extricate myself without causing it too much harm. After all, gargoyles were on the endangered cryptid list.

Thump.

My partner yelled, "How do we kill them?"

"We don't," I grunted as I used what little magic I had to give me the strength to heave the one pinning me into the air. Its wings, surprisingly translucent, fluttered as it slowed its descent to the floor.

I noticed Whiteclaw swinging a book at the one stalking him. Just one. Me? I had the one who pounced and another hemming me in from the side.

"Any suggestions on not dying?" Whiteclaw's retort.

I racked my brain for the little info I knew about gargoyles. They never came up as part of my studies due to their rarity. The best-known ones being those atop Notre Dame Cathedral. They'd been inert for more than a century. Dead or in a deep hibernation, no one could tell for sure.

"They're guardians," I stated.

"Which helps us how?" he exclaimed as he nimbly leaped to avoid the gargoyle rushing him.

I doubted I could do the same. I barely had enough magic to quickly erect a shield before my pair of gargoyles could hit me. A shield that shattered!

I grunted as the impact of a stone body sent me flying, losing my purse in the process. As I pushed myself to my feet, the gargoyle who knocked me dumped my purse out and grabbed the books I'd stashed. It handed one to the first gargoyle, and off they went, fluttering high enough to put them back on their shelves.

Maybe they weren't trying to kill us after all but simply wanted their library to remain intact. But if that were true, why had I been able to borrow books in the past?

I eyed the gargoyles as they turned from the shelves to face me once more. Their steady, thudding stomp let me know they weren't done. Since they'd easily shattered my shield, I tried a different spell. I flung magic at the gargoyles that should have frozen them.

Instead, it made their plodding steps quicker. My magic made them stronger. Not good.

"Um, I think we need to leave," I called out to Whiteclaw.

"Working on it," he grumbled. A quick glance showed him grappling with a gargoyle who, while much shorter in stature, definitely proved to be stronger given how it shoved him away from the stacks of books. In my direction, as it turned out.

With Whiteclaw at my side, we faced off against the advancing gargoyles.

"Suggestions?"

"I think we should go." Before the cryptids could shove us—or worse—I stepped onto the stairs and headed down into the tunnel, walking backwards. An awkward way of moving but it allowed me to keep an eye on the gargoyles until my partner followed. Then I got the lovely view of his ass.

We hit the bottom of the steps just as the gargoyles crowded the hatch opening.

Would they follow?

They didn't. The hatch closed. The gargoyles had done their job and removed the intruders.

"I don't think they wanted us in the library," he stated.

I snorted. "What gave it away?"

"How come you never mentioned the gargoyle guardians?"

"Because this is the first time they've come alive." I wrinkled my nose. "Probably because I never used magic in there before. It must have triggered their protective nature." And explained the drain on my power. They must have siphoned some from me to wake up.

"Well, at least we got what we came for."

At that, I shook my head. "They took the books before I even had a chance to really look at them."

"That sucks. Guess we'll have to take our chances with the internet."

"Maybe if we use a VPN, we'll throw anyone watching off track," I mused aloud.

"Your optimism is cute."

So was his ass, I thought as he took the lead back to the church. With only dregs of magic left, I created a weak ball of light that bobbed ahead of us and illuminated enough for me to admire the snug fit of his jeans and the taper of his waist from his broad shoulders. That's when I noticed a sheet of paper stuck out from his back pocket. Odd, because I didn't recall him having anything like that earlier. Yes, I'd looked at his ass a few times.

"What's that in your pocket?" I asked.

"Oh, I found it on the floor in the library, stuck under a bookcase, just before the attack." He tugged it free. "I didn't have a chance to read it. Kind of stashed it to have my hands free to fight."

"Can I see?" Because I'd been in that library numerous times. There'd never been a loose sheet of anything anywhere.

He handed it over, and I paused as I perused the tight script.

"What's it say?" he queried as I frowned.

"No idea. It's not an alphabet I know." In other words, not modern, which was the only one I spoke, read, or wrote.

"Let's figure it out once we get out of here."

The church remained empty, and we made our escape without notice or mishap. Once outside, though, I glanced at Whiteclaw. "Where are you staying?"

"Motel a few streets from the precinct."

"I assume the CA is paying for it?"

"Yeah." He then clued in on why I asked. "My location might be compromised." He glanced at me. "Your house would be, too."

The thought dropped a boulder in my stomach. I hated we even had to contemplate avoiding my home. Was that really how things were? "Maybe we're being overly paranoid."

"Really?" His raised eyebrow told me he didn't agree.

"The clerk didn't necessarily die because he'd seen the chimera and talked about it." I said it, but I didn't believe it. "And the cops writing the reports *could have* just been lazy." Nope, that one didn't ring true to my ears either.

"It's not worth taking the chance," my partner finished. "Unless you're rethinking your involvement. I'm sure Kowalski would let you off the case if you asked."

"Not a chance." I shook my head strongly. "I watched my precinct crumble from corruption before, and there's no way I'm going to turn a blind eye to it again."

"Okay, then. Any suggestions on where we can go?"

"Pretty much anywhere would work, so long as we don't tell anyone or leave a trace."

"If we want to stay off-grid, we'll need to pay for accommodations and everything else with cash. I'm gonna be honest and admit I have only like twenty bucks on me."

"And I have nothing since my purse is in that library." I wasn't about to risk pissing off the gargoyles going back to get it. I'd wait until they calmed down because, while I didn't give a crap about the bag itself, it still held not only the chimera case file, but also the one relating to my case.

"We're going to have to hit a bank and pull some dough if we want to rent a room."

"Not necessarily. I know a place we can hide out for free while we investigate."

The secret passage and the forgotten library weren't the only hidden gems I knew about. I'd found many covert sites in my time as a CA agent. The abandoned spots. The areas the homeless preferred. The locales everyone avoided.

I headed for the latter, paying a taxi driver with Whiteclaw's meager stash of cash. We had them drop us a half-mile from our destination: a lone house set amidst abandoned warehouses, looking pristine despite the neighborhood.

When I headed up the walkway, Whiteclaw paused. "This is where we're hiding? Who lives here?"

"No one."

"Are you sure?"

I could understand his skepticism. After all, the grass appeared freshly mowed, the picket fence an unsoiled white. "No one's lived here in more than forty years."

"Why not?" he asked as I headed up the three steps onto the porch.

"Because it's haunted."

Unlike many, he didn't scoff. "Haunted by who?"

"Not who. What." I remained purposely vague.

"Is it dangerous?"

"Yes." My lips curved. "Don't worry, though. I'll protect you."

He snorted. "Good to know."

I entered the house and called out, "Hey, Lenora. I'm back. Hope it's okay I brought company."

The occupant of the home materialized suddenly in the front hall. She wore a gown of diaphanous white. Her orange hair wisped and undulated as if underwater. Her eyes were black pits and her mouth a bright red.

To Whiteclaw's credit, he didn't faint, scream, or run away. He stared in shock at the banshee that floated in front of us.

"Um, hi?" He didn't sound all too certain. Don't tell me a super-agent, with all kinds of experience, never met a banshee before.

"Lenora, I'd like you to meet my partner, Koda Whiteclaw. Whiteclaw, this is Lenora, the owner of the house. Before you say something stupid, yes, she's a banshee. The CA is aware of her presence, but we've agreed to leave her alone so long as she behaves because of her former service to the bureau."

He glanced at me to exclaim, "She's a former CA agent?"

"One of the best," Lenora stated in a low whisper. "But that didn't save my family." A single tear tracked down her cheek, and I jumped in with an explanation before she went into hysterics.

"Enemies attacked while Lenora was away on CA business."

"Killed my babies," Lenora mournfully added.

"The grief transformed her into a banshee. She's been living here ever since."

"I'm sorry," he stated. "That's a devasting thing to have happen."

"It is," Lenora uttered on a high treble note.

Given I knew how easily she could go off, I hastened to distract. "Listen, sorry to barge in like this, but I wondered if we could stay here for a bit. My partner and I have stumbled across a dangerous situation and need to lie low."

"But of course." Lenora fluttered side to side in the hall. "Just don't use the children's room. I don't like it when people try to sleep in their beds." Her expression darkened.

Given the people who dared were usually squatters who broke in, the CA turned a blind eye when she scared them straight. Lenora had cured more drug addicts with her scream than any clinic managed.

"Thanks. Hopefully it won't be for more than a few days."

"If we're going to be here for a few, we'll need supplies," Whiteclaw stated.

"We have no more cash," I pointed out.

"I'm aware, which is why I'm going to pop out to get us some stuff."

His suggestion brought a frown. "If you use cards, you could be tracked," I reminded.

"We won't have a choice if we want to eat." True. So how to fix the problem?

"There is a food bank about five blocks east,"

Lenora mentioned. "You should be able to supply there."

"Which solves the hunger aspect. We still can't use the internet though," I mused aloud. "Making searches hard."

"You have access to the CA precinct, right?" Whiteclaw questioned.

"Yeah, but I thought we were avoiding the office."

"In the day, yes, but the night only has a skeleton shift. What if we went in and used the computers long enough to grab some info and then split?"

"If someone's bugged the computers, they'll see what we're doing."

"They already know we're looking. We should be able to get in and out, though, quickly enough to avoid trouble."

"It might work," I replied slowly. "Assuming whoever killed the clerk and is hiding the chimera isn't close by."

"It would be pretty bold to attack us there."

"So they'll wait until we leave."

"As if they could follow if we put our minds to it."

"There are spells that would muddy our tracks." I thought aloud.

"Why not set a trap instead?" Lenora's suggestion had me blinking.

"That isn't a bad idea," Whiteclaw agreed. "If someone is monitoring us, and looking to stop our investigation, then we could turn the tables."

My lips curved. "Go from hunted to hunter. Now why didn't I think of that?"

"Because you're too nice," Lenora tartly stated. "Back in my day, we weren't as gentle with criminals."

I didn't point out that her freedom to exist now only occurred because people felt sorry for her situation.

Whiteclaw raked fingers through his hair, disheveling it, then eyed his clothes with a grimace. "I look too nice for a food bank."

"I can help with that."

Before Lenora could explain, she threw herself at my partner. His eyes widened and his lips parted, but he didn't panic as the banshee ruined his garments, rending them in spots, somehow even dirtying them until he looked the part of a vagrant.

He shot a wry glance over his new look. "Guess I'm good to go. You'll be okay while I'm gone?"

I snorted. "Been fine for thirty-five years now. Pretty sure I can survive a few hours on my own. Besides, I've got Lenora."

The banshee dipped and rolled as she chirped, "This is my house. Intruders aren't welcome."

"In that case, I'll be back in a few."

"Wait." I halted him before he could leave. "Give me that sheet of paper you found. I'll examine it while you're gone."

"I thought you couldn't read it," he stated as he handed it over.

"I can't, but maybe there's a way to decipher it."

"Sounds good. Stay safe." The last thing he said before heading out the door.

As it closed, I restrained an urge to follow. He'd be fine on his own. Always had been. So why did it bother me all of a sudden?

It didn't. I was just being dumb. Piece of paper in hand, I strode in the direction of the kitchen, a hovering banshee keeping close.

"What's the piece of paper from? Is it important?" Lenora asked.

"I don't know. Not yet. We found it in a secret library after casting a spell for information on a chimera."

"Oh, I'll bet the gargoyles didn't like that."

Her comment led to me doing a double-take. "Hold on, you know about them and the books?"

"Oh yes. Found it while tracking down a bogey."

"How come there's no record of it?"

"Because some secrets are best kept hidden," Lenora stated. "Not to mention, I kind of liked having exclusive access to it."

Her argument closely resembled mine.

"How come the gargoyles wouldn't let me take any of the books? In the past, it was never an issue."

"Let me guess. You used magic."

"How do you know?"

"Because I did the same thing," Lenora admitted with a giggle. "I was looking to see if there were any books on potions. I used to love dabbling. It woke up the gargoyles. I tried returning afterwards, but apparently, a little bit of magic goes a long way. Enough about those stony book guardians. Tell me more about this chimera."

"Not much to tell. Thus far, the only thing I know for sure is she escaped a prison last year after being incarcerated for more than thirty years."

"Why was she imprisoned?" Lenora's next query.

"We were told 'crimes against humanity,' but as to specifics, no idea. The file we were given on her was almost entirely redacted. We don't even have a name."

"How odd. Why would anyone do that?" Lenora mused aloud as she floated horizontally, almost touching the ceiling.

"I don't know. It makes no sense."

"Unless her crime was so heinous they wanted no one to repeat it."

"I guess that's a possibility." Yet it didn't feel right. "I also don't understand why someone would be hiding everything about her now. Why is no one on the internet talking about magical fires? Why did the security footage go missing? Why did someone kill the clerk who saw her?"

Then because Lenora still listened, I added, "Apparently, there's a bounty on her head."

"Meaning there is someone still alive from that time who wants vengeance. Do you know who?"

I shook my head. "They posted the reward anonymously. But here's the strange part. They want her delivered alive."

"Not so strange. Most likely they want to torture

and kill her themselves." If anyone could understand that desire, it would be Lenora. "Sounds to me like there's at least one party trying to protect her by redacting files and concealing her movement and another who wants her brought out into the open. You should speak with them."

"Trust me, I've thought about it." My lips turned down. "The problem is, they're communicating on the dark web, and it's highly unlikely they'll volunteer to talk to CA agents. I figure the only way to get them to agree to meet is by offering them information on the chimera, but I don't have anything juicy enough to dangle."

"What about the sheet of paper you found in the library?" Lenora asked, reminding me I clutched it.

"I hardly doubt an old page from a book is going to help." Still, I had some hope considering it had appeared after I cast the spell.

I smoothed it out on the table and stared at it. It didn't make the writing any clearer. I sent a prayer to Hekate. *Oh goddess, if you're listening, I don't suppose you'd give me the power to translate?*

No reply.

How about a refill on magic so I can cast a spell to decipher?

Still nothing.

I sighed. Hopefully my magic would regenerate enough on its own before I needed it again.

Lenora floated above the table, over the sheet of paper. "How interesting. This is a page from a diary."

The comment had me eyeing her in surprise. "You can read it?"

"Oh yes. I took linguistics in college. It's in ancient Greek. One of the seven languages I know."

Excitement filled me. "What does it say?"

"Let's see..." Her voice took on a monotone quality as she recited. "It starts off mid-thought and sentence. ...won't leave me alone. I've moved yet again and still *he*"—Lenora added an inflection to the word—"pursues. How does *he* keep finding me? Why won't *he* take no for an answer? Surely there is another that would be pleased by *his* attention. I want nothing more than for *him* to leave me alone. Especially now that I've met my true love. The danger is great. If *he* were to find out my heart belonged to another, I fear what will happen. I've tried to tell my love to leave. To find another. He refuses. He is so brave. Determined to stand by my side. He held me as I sobbed and said goodbye to another home. Promised me that one day we'd be free to live in happiness. I wish I had my love's optimism. I am so tired of running. So tired of having to move one place after another lest *he* get a piece of me. If *he* does, I'm doomed. My fate will be worse than death. Surely there is a way to stop someone like him? I can only hope my love's latest quest proves fruitful. Else I fear for the life growing within me."

Lenora stopped.

"That's it?"

"Yes."

"Well, that wasn't useful," I muttered. Not a single

word about a chimera. Just a saga of a woman with a stalker. I really wished I'd been able to keep the books the gargoyles took from me.

"You say you found this in the library?" Lenora queried, once more floating by the ceiling.

"Koda did. He said it was the floor, stuck under a bookcase, which was odd because I don't recall seeing it there before." Then again, it was possible that someone else knew about the library and had dropped it.

"Odd. This missive is only a few decades old."

My tapping fingers paused. "I thought you said it was in ancient Greek."

"It is, but the paper? It's modern, as is the ink used to write it."

I leaned forward to stare and cursed. "How did I not realize that?"

"Because you made an assumption."

"How did it end up in that hidden library?"

Lenora shrugged. "I often wondered if the gargoyles, or some kind of latent spell, continued to seek out texts even after the library fell into disuse."

Interesting, but not the mystery I needed to solve today. Out of curiosity, I asked Lenora, "I don't suppose you know what color a chimera's flames are?"

"What a strange thing to ask. Blue, of course," Lenora replied, matter-of-factly.

The reply startled. "Are you sure?"

"Oh yes. As part of my training, I spent some time in Greece and actually met a chimera while I was there. Lovely woman with the most intense eyes. One of them a bright blue, just like her hair, the other dark as night."

"Is that a common trait?" Because I couldn't help but think of that partial image I'd captured from the clerk's memories.

"I wouldn't know. She's the only chimera I ever met. I do believe, though, that mismatched eyes are a species thing for them."

"Do you recall her name?"

"Of course, it's..." Lenora paused her fluttering and frowned. "Well, this is embarrassing. I can't seem to remember. Is it important?"

"Probably not." Even if the chimera Lenora met was the same one I chased, a name wouldn't help if her entire existence had been wiped.

"What's your plan?" Lenora asked.

"I'm not sure." We'd gotten as far as agreeing that Koda should pick up some food, and then possibly visit the CA office that night. Maybe even setting a trap for anyone coming after us.

Dangling ourselves as bait wasn't my favorite idea. However, I might not have a choice if I wanted to shake a clue loose. Once Whiteclaw returned we could discuss how we'd go about drawing out anyone looking to stop our investigation.

At least that was my plan until Lenora asked, "Why did you ask about the color of the chimera's flames?"

"Because the reports I've read on the fires didn't

mention it, and I've recently learned that one of the fires supposedly caused by her was purple."

"Well then it can't have been your chimera. What about the other fires she supposedly set? What color were they?"

"I don't know." But I suddenly realized I knew who to talk to that might.

CHAPTER 7

Koda left the safe house—an oxymoron considering the banshee inhabitant—at a quick clip. While he'd not lied about getting them food, he had an ulterior motive for wanting to put distance between him and his partner. He needed to use his phone and could only do that away from Marissa, so anyone possibly tracking him through it wouldn't be led straight to her.

Koda planned to call Abe. Not returning to the office that afternoon and not checking in with the boss would alert the precinct that something was off. If he didn't touch base soon, Kowalski would have all of CA looking for their asses.

Only once he'd walked a few miles did Koda insert his battery into his phone and make a call.

Abe answered right away. "Where are you? No one's seen or heard from you since this morning, and you haven't been replying to my messages."

"Shit happened, and so we went off-grid."

"We? You're with Agent Smith?" Abe's sharp query.

"Yeah."

"What happened? Why are you flying under the radar?"

"Yesterday we went to question a witness to the fire in the cell phone shop."

Kowalski took a second to answer, and Koda knew the man was debating whether to grill him on why they'd been there instead of investigating the fires he'd assigned, or to trust Whiteclaw's methods and just let him be. Thankfully, the latter won out. "And did he have anything to say?"

"Not much." Koda glanced at the blue sky, deciding how much he wanted to say. He didn't have an issue with Abe, that man had earned his trust, however, he did wonder if anyone eavesdropped on the call. At the same time, why not reveal what they'd discovered. If he and Marissa were targets already, then sharing what they knew wasn't going to change that now. "We did get a partial image of the woman who robbed the store, and we learned there were twenty minutes between her leaving and the fire starting. Otherwise, nothing else of real use. Still, someone must have been worried because the clerk we talked to was killed last night."

"By the chimera?"

"Unlikely, given the span of time between the witness talking to the police and then to us. Besides, the report had him dead of a gunshot wound, not fire."

"Probably a robbery gone wrong."

"That's what the reports said." *It's what someone wants us to believe.* He didn't share this suspicion with Abe.

"What's the status on your search for related arsons? Any leads?"

"No." He tactfully avoided informing Abe that they'd yet to look into that. "We're dredging up more questions than answers. Such as the fact the chimera has a bounty on her head."

"Not surprising. She's a wanted criminal."

"This has nothing to do with apprehending her to return to prison, though. The person paying wants her delivered alive."

"Who?" Abe sharply queried.

"No clue. It's a mystery, just like that useless file you gave us with the blacked-out information. I don't suppose you've been able to dig up anything useful for us?"

"Unfortunately, no."

"Why would the CA have redacted the charges against her?" he asked. "Or her name for that matter?"

"No idea." Abe's non-answers would have frustrated Koda more if he didn't grasp the complications of bureaucracy. Just because Kowalski led a precinct didn't mean he had immediate access to information from those higher up in the CA.

"Then how did the CA connect her to the fires in the first place?" He found himself parroting Smith's argument.

"Let's just say I received an inside tip."

"Meaning someone else is monitoring her actions. Who?"

"I can't say. Let's just say they're eager for her to be found."

"Is it someone in the CA?"

"I'm afraid that's privileged information. Sorry."

That had Koda grinding his teeth. "Given the lengths someone is going to keep her under wraps, you might want to be careful."

"You're sounding a little paranoid," Abe cajoled.

"More like cautious. Something about this case isn't adding up."

"I have faith in you and Agent Smith. You're both smart and tenacious. Why do you think I chose you to work on this?" Abe paused before saying, "What's your next move? Any idea of where the chimera might have gone after the last fire?"

"No. But we're working on it." He didn't mention the plan to use themselves as bait to draw out the person—or cryptid—that might have killed the clerk. Maybe they were being paranoid and it was just a coincidence he died right after their visit.

"How do I get a hold of you? Are you at the hotel or Marissa's place?" Abe queried.

"Neither. She worried about us being spied upon or attacked. So we're staying somewhere off the main beat."

"If you're that worried, the office can provide extra agents as backup."

"We're fine." He didn't mention the fact Smith worried the CA department still had rats.

Abe caught on anyhow. "You don't have to worry about their integrity. I've vetted them all at this point. They're good."

"I'm sure they are, but for the moment, we're going to work this together. If we need more help, we'll let you know."

"This place you're staying at, it's secure?"

"Of sorts, so long as we don't piss off the owner," he joked. He still couldn't wrap his head around the fact a banshee was allowed to live essentially free of restraint. Most were incarcerated or exorcised because of their murderous predilection.

"Good. Try to keep me apprised of the situation."

"Will do."

Koda hung up and pulled the battery from his phone before quickly making his way out of the area. Was Abe correct about them being paranoid? Technically, they'd not been directly attacked or threatened. The library thing with the gargoyles had nothing to do with the current case.

Still, it didn't hurt to be cautious. He hit the food bank and made a note of its address so he could make a cash donation later to cover what he took, plus some. By the time he returned to the house, taking a circuitous route despite seeing no one, dusk had settled. The porch light of the banshee's home provided a beacon on an otherwise very dark street.

He knocked because it seemed rude to just walk in.

The door swung open, and Koda stepped in to see Lenora floating in the hall wringing her hands. "About time you returned. I couldn't talk her out of it."

"Talk Marissa out of what?"

"Going to talk to the firefighters."

He set the box of groceries down. "Dare I ask why?"

"To ask them about the color of the fires they've seen lately. She also said something about contacting some firefighters in other towns to pose the same question."

"And why did she suddenly feel a need to do that?"

"Something about purple fire and the chimera. Which makes no sense since their kind makes blue flames."

"Wait, the chimera's fire burns blue?"

"Don't tell me you didn't know that either." Lenora rolled her eyes as she floated in lazy eights in the front hall. "Exactly what are they teaching agents these days?"

"How long ago did she leave?"

"Maybe an hour after you."

"Did she mention how she'd be talking to the firefighters? Was she calling them? Going to see them in person?"

Lenora shrugged. "She just said tell him—as in you—to wait here and she'd be back soon."

Soon could mean any number of things. One hour. Two…

He wondered how long he should wait before he

worried. Actually, he already worried because, if it were true and the chimera's burned blue, then that meant the cell phone store fire had been set by someone other than the chimera. Hell, the woman seen exiting could have been anyone. It wasn't as if they had a picture to compare, only the word of whatever CA agent who claimed to detect chimera essence at the location. It also raised an interesting question: Why was someone trying to frame the chimera for arson?

Something in the whole equation didn't add up. He just needed to figure it out. But now he understood what Marissa sought. Proof of fires actually set by the chimera. Because if the flames were anything but blue, then they were chasing the wrong arsonist.

Sitting around didn't suit Koda, especially as the evening progressed with no sign of Smith. A woman with too much bravery, unafraid to investigate on her own. No wonder Abe wanted her partnered with someone. She couldn't just be going off and... what? Doing just as he had. Furthering their investigation. Why did he think it okay for him to leave but not her?

He'd never shown misogynistic tendencies before, so what about Smith was different? Why did he want her working with him, closely, as in his line of vision? He had one answer that he didn't particularly care for. The mating urge. Something he'd thought himself immune to. After all, that sudden irresistible attraction to someone happened to other people, not him. Or so he'd always thought. Now, with his anxiety peaking because he had no idea where to find his partner, he had to wonder if he'd been afflicted.

Whatever the reason, as the evening progressed, his worry compounded—*What if she's hurt? Stuck? Captured?* He'd just about convinced himself to go looking when she entered the house.

"I'm back," Smith chirped as he launched himself out of a living room chair.

"About time," he barked.

"Did you miss me?" she teased.

Yes, but instead, he whined, "We're supposed to be a team."

"Teams are allowed to research things on their own. You did your thing, I did mine. No harm."

"No harm except I had no idea where you were or when to expect you back."

"Sorry. I would have called, but the whole 'my phone is currently in the custody of angry gargoyles' thing made it kind of hard. Now instead of being a berating daddy, why don't you ask me what I found out?"

He wanted to keep haranguing and had to remind himself she was a grown-ass woman and an accomplished agent. She knew how to do her job, so he needed to stop being so goddamned overprotective. And to the tiny inner voice that asked, no, he would not be peeing on her. Or biting. Or doing the horizontal tango. And the same went for doggy style.

"Where did you go, and what did you discover?" he

growled as he followed her into the kitchen, doing his best to not picture that round ass of hers in the air.

She dug into the box of food as she replied. "I went to the nearby fire station, where a friend of mine works. I wanted to get some info from the source. In unfortunate news, there have been two recent local fires attributed to magic, but they burned purple, not blue, which is the—"

"Color the chimera casts."

"Wait, how do you know the chimera casts blue?"

"Lenora told me." He waved a hand. "So what do we know about these fires? I take it you asked."

"I did. Lucky for me Rick was—"

"Who's Rick?" he blurted out, unable to stop the spurt of jealousy that suddenly infused his body.

"Pal of mine who is a firefighter. Anyhow, of the two new purple fires, one was at a motel off the highway, and the other in an abandoned mall."

"Not a lot to go off of. Mall fire could be from any magic hooligans messing around. Same for the motel, really."

"Right. We won't know for sure if it's related to our others until we can get one of those scryers to see if they can detect chimera essence."

"Did *Rick* find anything else for you?"

"Yes, actually." She spoke with a bright smile that Koda could only hope was for the fact that they had new evidence, and not from thinking about Rick. "He had some connections at the department that worked on the mobile phone store fire. Of interest, not one firefighter who showed up to the cell phone store fire claimed to have seen any blue flames."

"We already knew that from the video footage we saw."

"Never hurts to confirm," Marissa stated. "But knowing that, it does raise a question. Why have CA agents claimed the chimera is responsible for these four fires?"

"She's an escaped prisoner with a fire power, and a scryer picked up her essence in the area. Could be they drew a connection and didn't know about the blue flames."

"Maybe." She shrugged. "Anyhow, Rick was then kind enough to do a search to see if we could find any other blue or purple fires since the prison break last year. Not a single blue reported one since the chimera's escape, but purple? There's been at least a dozen in the past six months. Of special interest, once Rick inputted the addresses into a map on his computer, I noticed they form a zigzag that starts from the prison where the chimera escaped, heading in what seems like the direction of this town."

"Which makes it more likely that the mall fire and the hotel fire are connected, and the chimera was headed here all along."

"The purple fire starter was headed here," Marissa corrected. "And yes, it appears that way, or her destination lies past us. In either case, it explains why Kowalski worried she'd be hitting our town soon."

"But why here?"

She shrugged. "I assume there's something or someone she wants in the area."

"Which will be almost impossible to figure out given the redaction of her file."

"I wish I still had it," she grumbled. "I wonder if a spell of revelation would have let us read the full report."

"It was printed that way, so highly unlikely."

"Says you," she pouted. "I'd like to think my magic might have been able to see through it."

"Wishful thinking." He changed the subject. "Abe will be happy to learn that he was right about the fires headed this way."

"He already knows," her flat reply.

"What do you mean he knows?"

She pressed her lips together before explaining. "The fire station had already informed the CA about the purple fires, and I knew that Abe would be starting to get concerned about not hearing from us, so I used Rick's VPN to drop Abe a message and let him know we were on top of things. I'm sorry, I know we agreed to not share info but—"

"Don't be sorry. I also spoke with Abe while I was out." He cut her off before she continued on her guilt-fueled apology.

"You did?" She blinked at him in surprise before a smile bloomed. "I guess great minds do think alike."

"I guess so." The thought warmed him as much as her smile did.

"How much of our investigation did you share with him?"

"Not too much since I worried his phone might be compromised. He's aware of what we learned from the clerk and the bounty."

"How did he react?" She looked wary, as though she worried they might be in trouble.

"Interested but not excitable. Accepting that we're choosing to lie low."

She nodded, relieved. "Typical Kowalski."

"Still want to hit CA headquarters tonight?"

She yawned. "Maybe after a power nap? It's been a long day."

"Probably best we wait until tomorrow night, then. We'll be able to plan how we want to handle it."

"You mean lay the trap for whoever might be watching us."

"Assuming someone is."

"Given our current case, I'd say that's a given. Someone wants the chimera found as much as someone else doesn't. At this point, I think locating either one of them might advance our current task."

"I agree."

"Good. I'll talk to you in the morning, then. Night." She headed off, taking the stairs to the second floor.

His gaze went to the ceiling as if he could track her steps. Not just could, he did.

Lenora drifted down to murmur, "She's in the guest bed, which is big enough for two."

The suggestion startled. "We're not lovers."

"You will be." Lenora managed to sound certain.

"We're just partners."

"So were my husband and I until we married." Her lips turned down and trembled as she added, "They executed him as he stood in front of our children trying to defend them."

"Who did that to your family?" he asked.

"A criminal." Her mouth curled in derision, and her hair whipped in agitation as her voice rose in pitch. "I'd arrested him for illegal cryptid trafficking. A judge set him free on bail. He chose to take his anger out on my poor babies."

"You killed him." He stated, not asked.

"Oh yes. He was the first to hear my scream." The banshee grinned, and it gave him a shiver, for the violence—and madness—were plain to see.

"Why come back here?" he wondered aloud. "Wouldn't your grief be less somewhere with no memories?"

"I don't want to forget," Lenora's indignant reply.

"Then you're braver than most."

"And you are afraid of a little witch," cackled Lenora.

"Not afraid." Just leery of his sudden intense interest.

"Where should I sleep?" he asked to change the subject.

"There is only one guest bed."

"Which is already occupied," he reminded.

"It's big enough, as stated, for two, but if you insist

on being stubborn, then the couch should be able to accommodate."

He grimaced. He'd sat on it earlier. Firm, narrow but at least long enough for his frame. He'd slept on worse.

The uncomfortable sofa couldn't be blamed for his restlessness though. He kept staring at the ceiling, knowing she slumbered directly above. And he knew this despite having not visited the second floor. Call it instinct. Or the animal within. He found himself much too aware of Marissa.

And horny too.

His cock kept asking him for some help, but he worried Lenora would catch him. She flitted in and out of the living room at random, peering out the windows before drifting off again.

He held in a sigh as he shifted for the umpteenth time on the couch. Sleep remained elusive, and thus, when he heard a small cry, he arose instantly and found himself halfway up the stairs before it occurred to him that perhaps he should slow down before barging in on Marissa.

What if rather than being attacked, she had a bad dream?

A noise like that could also be a sign she masturbated.

Dirty, wishful thinking, still the reasoning slowed his steps on the second-floor landing and walked quietly to the door at the end of the hall. He pressed his ear to the panel and listened.

Heard nothing at first then a soft moan. Not one of pleasure, though. It raised the hairs on his nape.

He put his hand to the knob on the door and hissed, as it burned his palm. He snatched it back and shook it as if that would cure the blister forming. He smelled and saw no sign of smoke, but the knob wouldn't be scalding for no reason. He stripped his shirt and wrapped it around the knob before turning it again.

Expecting to see an inferno, he stumbled and halted in surprise at the threshold of the room. For one, he didn't find any fire. Not a real blaze at any rate, but definite heat oozed from the space. It scorched the skin and seared the lungs as he breathed in.

The bed, a queen-sized four-poster held a flowered comforter, wreathed in ghostly flames. They licked around the woman lying on the mattress, her eyes closed, her face slack in repose.

"Smith?" He murmured her name softly, not wanting to startle her. What happened? Dream, nightmare, or something else? The air tingled with static, indicating magic at play.

"No." Her head flapped to the side. She moaned, and the ghost flames rose in response.

Despite them being new acquaintances, he used her first name to see if she might respond better. "Marissa, wake up."

She trembled under the covers, and then she floated. Wraithlike and unresponsive, her body lifted from the mattress, and despite the flames not being real, her clothing, a nightgown that seemed out of date, burned. It fell in tatters and ash to the mattress below, leaving her nude.

He should have looked away. Should have shouted, grabbed her for a shake, even called Lenora for help.

Instead, he stared.

He knew it was wrong, but damn! The woman had a slamming body, and a man only had so much willpower. It took all of his to avert his gaze.

This couldn't be good. He had to wake her. He tried to take a step forward, only to recoil with a gasp as a wall of heat slammed him.

"What's going on?" Lenora shrieked. "Why is the bed on fire?"

"I think Marissa is having a nightmare and her magic is reacting." His grim reply as he tried to figure out how to help her.

"Oh dear. Oh dear." Lenora flitted around the room, unaffected by the heat.

"Wake her up," he suggested since Lenora could at least get close without harm.

Lenora halted midair to blink at him before diving in a swoop that had her brushing past Marissa's nude form. Again and again, Lenora tried to subtly wake before she finally halted above the witch and uttered a piercing shriek that sent him to his knees.

Ow.

It hurt his ears, but at least it woke Marissa. She went to sit bolt upright, and whatever magic fueled her levitation failed. She slammed into the bed and bounced before she bounded to her feet, where she stood gloriously naked atop the mattress.

"What's happened?" she huffed, fists raised ready to fight.

He pushed himself to his feet. "You were on fire... of sorts. It was weird though. I could feel heat, and it destroyed your gown, but you appear unharmed and nothing else burned."

"Not again," she muttered, glancing down at her nude body. Her cheeks turned pink. "Um."

Lenora replied before Marissa could. "I'll get you another nightgown."

His cue to leave, only he kept standing there, trying to look her in the eye and not any lower.

"You okay?" he asked.

"Just embarrassed. I haven't had one of the fire dreams in years."

"What exactly is a fire dream?"

Her lips pursed. "It's a memory. Or so I assume. I was orphaned at a young age. Parents unknown. Authorities found me in the remains of a house that burned down."

"You were the only survivor?" he queried.

"Yes. There was much argument about if I actually lived in that house or was placed there once the fire died down."

"Why would anyone do that?"

She rolled her shoulders as she sat down, hiding most of her body.

Pity.

"I've heard a few theories to explain how they found me. Some thought I was abandoned on purpose. That whoever had custody of me saw the ruins and knew emergency crews would be by and find me. Others claim I was the fire starter and killed my family. I didn't," she amended. "They never found any bodies."

"What do you remember?"

"Nothing." She shook her head. "My memories begin the moment they plucked me from those ashes."

"Give her this." Lenora swooped into the room, dropped a nightgown in front of him, and flitted off.

He snared the fabric, something slinkier than before. He held it out but knew he didn't have the reach to hand it over. It meant walking farther into the room, closer to the bed, closer to her.

Marissa leaned forward, and this time he couldn't stop his eyes from following the sway of her breasts as she bent to snare the nightgown from his hand.

"Thanks." She proceeded to drop the gown over her head, and only once it hit her calves—and hid her luscious frame—did she sigh. "That's better. Nothing like showing your partner the goods less than a week on the job."

"Would you feel better if I exposed myself so we're even?"

"Sure." She knelt on the bed, dressed in the gown, and yet she might as well have remained naked given how it hugged her curves and the tips of her nipples poked through the fabric. "Let's go. Show me the goods."

His eyes widened. "Wait, I was only kidding."

"I'm not. You've seen me naked. Your turn." She waved a hand and waited.

He ducked his head, and his cheeks flooded with heat. "I don't think that's a good idea."

"Why not? Afraid I'll ogle."

No, he feared doing something he couldn't take back, like dragging her into his arms for a kiss.

"More that I'll embarrass myself. It's been a while since I've been with someone. I wouldn't want to shock you." He had a semi hard-on that he didn't want her to see.

"That small?"

His mouth rounded. "No."

"Says you." She swung her legs over the edge of the bed. "Let's see it."

"I'd really rather not."

"Well, you'd better get a new partner then because I can't work with you knowing you've seen me in the buff."

"How does seeing me naked fix that?"

Her lips quirked. "Because then we'd be even."

"My shirt is off." He pointed out the obvious.

"But not your pants."

"You're really serious."

"Yup." She stood. "So what's it going to be? Partners? Or am I working solo again?"

"This is dumb," he grumbled as his hands went to the button on his jeans.

"It's just nudity. You're a shifter. This shouldn't be such an issue."

"I'm private about such things."

"So am I," she countered as he undid the next two buttons on his fly.

It took a deep breath and staring at the upper part of the wall before he could shove his pants down his thighs.

"Underpants too."

He grabbed them and whipped them down to his ankles. "Happy?"

"All the way off," she stated, hopping off the bed and standing closer to him.

Rather than argue, he kicked his pants and underpants to the side, planted his hands on his hips, and pursed his lips.

She cocked her head and stared. She didn't even try to look at his face. She stared at his cock. His cock noticed, even lifted its head to say hello.

And what did she do? Licked her lips. "Not bad, Whiteclaw."

His cock jutted and pointed in her direction. "You better not whine about me sexually harassing you because this"—he gestured to his erection—"is not my fault."

"You're right. It's mine." Her grin warmed him through and through. "Why, Agent Whiteclaw, I do believe you find me attractive."

"As if there was any doubt," he grumbled.

She took a step closer. "You're nothing like I first expected."

"What did you expect?"

"Well, seeing as how the first time I saw you, an entourage stroked your ego, I expected you to be pompous."

He snorted. "People are weird around me because of the ogre situation from a few years ago."

She blinked. "Wait, that was you that wrestled into submission that rampaging ogre in Scottsdale?"

"Yup."

Her gaze went to his arms, the biceps defined but not overtly so. "Nice job."

"I guess. I didn't actually go there to wrangle the ogre. I was supposed to locate a missing artifact from a museum."

"You're smaller than I would have expected from the stories."

"You should never put any credence in rumors."

"Except for the one saying you're hung like a satyr."

"What?" He blinked at her. "Who's saying that?"

Once more, her lips curved in a way that had his cock aching. "Just something I heard. Turns out it's true."

The comment only made his face hotter and his dick harder. "Okay, now that we've ogled each other, can I get dressed?"

"I suppose," she huffed. Then laughed. "The look on your face is priceless."

"And what look is that?"

She took a step closer, close enough she had to tilt her head and he could have reached out easily to drag her close. "Embarrassment, a bit of anger, but also lust. Nice to know I've still got it at thirty-five."

"You're hot as fuck, and you know it."

Her lips pursed. "It's actually been a while since anyone noticed. I don't date much."

"Me either. The job keeps me busy."

"It does," she agreed. "People outside the CA agency don't understand."

"They want to know why you're late or all bruised up."

"Then they tell you to get a nice job, a safe job."

He chuckled. "As if I'd change my life."

"Someone who gets it," she murmured.

Oh, he did. It was why his relationships never lasted.

Despite them not speaking, they drew closer. Him bending down, her leaning up. The kiss hit him like a jolt. A soft press of her lips to his. A shock that rocked him head to toe.

Before he could react—as in drag her close and thoroughly embrace her—she drew back. "I'm sorry. That was wrong of me. You should get dressed."

As if he could stuff his turgid cock back into his pants. He did his best but had to leave them partially unbuttoned. She gazed out a window as he said, "Good night, Agent Smith."

To his surprise, she murmured, "Call me Marissa."

"Good night, Marissa."

"Sweet dreams, Koda."

The couch wasn't to blame for his inability to sleep. The woman upstairs had left him hard and aching. Also confused. He didn't understand his insane attraction to her.

His inability to slumber wasn't aided by Lenora's lurking and tsking. "You really don't know how to seduce, do you? You had her. What happened? Why are you back on the couch?"

"We barely know each other."

"And? I knew my husband only a day before I decided I would marry him."

Marry? They'd just met. This was simply lust. So explain then the certainty that if they did sleep together, it might turn into forever.

CHAPTER 8

It took me forever to fall back asleep thanks to a myriad of thoughts. Fear of the dream flames returning. Wondering what my partner thought about me after witnessing my episode. Wondering what my partner thought about my naked body and the kiss we shared... I even imagined what might have happened if we'd kept kissing.

I woke the next day grumpy—and horny.

The latter caused the former, and I blamed Koda's actions the night before. First the man had stared at me, making me tingle in naughty places, and then he purposely didn't ogle me at all. Annoying because when his gaze devoured me like a man starving—eyeing me as if I were the yummiest thing ever—I'd never felt more desirable. When he ignored me, I'd been miffed, hence my demand he strip, which he obeyed. I'd honestly expected him to tell me to fuck off. But he didn't. He dropped his drawers and showed me an epic body, his abs nicely toned, his chest bare of hair, his arms defined, and his cock...

Damn.

Like seriously. Damn.

At that point, I'd expected him to pull a move. What naked guy wouldn't?

Koda apparently had more self-control than most. Most guys would have correctly read my kiss as an invitation. The spark he'd ignited had me ready to do more than taste his lips. But did the man sweep me off my feet to bed?

Nope. When I said, 'Oops sorry,' he'd dressed and left without any attempt at seduction. I might have been more miffed if I'd not seen his difficulty in getting his pants closed. While I had my back to him, the reflection in the window showed his struggle. His erection refused to subside, and that longing look he shot in my direction? He wanted me; he just didn't act.

Why?

Did he have a girlfriend or someone special? The very thought made me see red.

It couldn't be about work. The CA allowed fraternization so long as it didn't affect our performance. Most times, dating or married couples were split up so as to avoid conflict of interest.

Could be shyness. Unlikely but, hey, some guys struggled making moves.

Or maybe he just didn't like me. My body, yes, but perhaps my personality turned him off. It wouldn't be the first time.

I hated not knowing. Hated being tingly and not in a place where I could do something about it. Yes, I could have used my fingers, but honestly, I'd gotten spoiled when it came to masturbation. I liked my vibrating dildo with its clit tickler if I couldn't have the real thing.

When I finally decided to roll my tired ass out of bed, I grimaced in the mirror at the bags under my eyes. Pretty girl. Not!

I dressed before I headed downstairs, only to make a face at breakfast. Cereal and powdered milk.

A grim-faced Koda didn't look impressed as he shoveled it into his mouth. "Morning," he stated.

"Thank you for not saying good, because that was the worst night of sleep," I complained. I almost told him he was to blame.

"There's coffee," he indicated. "There's extra powdered milk in the fridge and sugar cubes in the bowl by the coffee maker." The appliances in the home, while old, remained in excellent working condition, built in a time when longevity and quality mattered.

"I like my coffee strong." *Just like my men*, a comment I kept to myself. I poured myself a mug and sat in the seat across from Koda. "Where's Lenora lurking?"

"No idea. Haven't seen her since last night." He shoveled more cereal into his mouth. A mouth I'd kissed. A mouth that would look oh-so-good on certain parts of my body.

I must have stared overly long because he shifted in his seat and his cheeks took on a ruddy hue.

I took a sip of coffee before mumbling. "What's our plan today?"

"I'm thinking we hit the CA office to set our trap in motion."

"Weren't we supposed to wait until night?" I reminded.

"Change of plan. I say we go in broad daylight."

"Need some adulation from your fans?" I'd not forgotten his groupies the first day we met.

"Fuck no," he exclaimed. "I thought it might be revealing to see who takes an interest in what we're doing."

"In case there's a mole." His logic made sense. "I'm good with the change in plan. Either way, we were going to have to be careful when we leave to not be followed."

"Assuming anyone does."

The comment led to me blurting out, "You no longer think we're in danger." Something I'd been wondering myself. Had I been too hasty with my assumption? One dead clerk didn't mean a murder conspiracy.

"I think it would be good to know for sure. Add to that we are both trained agents. Taking down bad people is what we do."

"Agreed. When do we leave?" Because sitting around twiddling my thumbs didn't appeal.

"Now?"

"Thank fuck." I dropped the mug of shitty coffee. "Let's get some real food on the way in."

"I have no cash left."

"We'll put it on your card until I can grab mine, but let's wait until we're at least a mile out from here in case we decide to come back tonight."

Since Lenora remained out of sight, I left her a note. A basic one. *Gone to work. Might return later. Thanks for your hospitality.*

We left the banshee house, our pace steady. Only as we got a few blocks away—leaving behind the desolation of that abandoned area—did Koda clear his throat.

"I don't suppose we could swing by my hotel so I can change."

"What's wrong? Afraid the people in the office will think you're doing the morning-after walk of shame?" I teased.

"I'm more concerned with the fact that I look like, well..." He gestured from his shirt to his pants, which were still dirty and holey from the job Lenora had done on them. "But besides that, yeah. We left together and are now returning together in the same clothes."

"Good point." Office gossip could be worse than a beating by a misbehaving cryptid. My lips pinched. "In that case, we should hit my place too."

With that decided, he connected his phone and ordered us a ride. Thankfully, he didn't quibble about using his credit card. My purse remained in the library, along with my wallet and cell. In good news, I kept a hide-a-key for my house and a spare bank card and Visa because, in my line of work, losing my wallet happened more often than I liked. Ever been goo-ed by a mutant frog? Stuff burned through anything nonorganic instantly.

Given our route, we hit Koda's hotel first, a basic chain with a generic exterior and rooms to match. When Koda opened the door to his, I found myself surprised at the mess. He didn't seem like the type to toss his shit around.

Because he wasn't.

"Someone riffled through my stuff," he grimly noted as he glanced around.

"Is anything missing?"

"Hard to tell. I mean they might have stolen a pair of socks or something. I didn't exactly pay attention when I packed. At least I didn't leave anything of value in the room."

"Still sucks," I commiserated.

"It happens."

"What you should be asking is, were you specifically targeted or just a victim of location?"

His lips pursed. "A good question." He began to pile the strewn items on the bed, and I helped him, discovering he had a love for black briefs, black socks, and button-up shirts. Also jeans. Lots and lots of jeans.

When he hit the bathroom to change, I sat crosslegged on the floor with my hands upraised on my knees. My magic had partially regenerated overnight, and so I had the power to craft a spell.

Koda emerged from the bathroom just as I finished casting. A haze settled over his room, a faint overlay that showed the room in the past when his bed remained neatly made and his suitcase sat open on the little doohickey they put in rooms specially for them. In this vision, the door opened and someone entered. Someone who appeared as a blur.

"Can you fix the focus?" Koda murmured.

"I'm trying." I frowned as I pushed more juice into the spell, but while everything else from that rewind got clearer, the figure remained an indistinct smudge that dumped out the suitcase before searching in the drawers, yanking back sheets, and even checking under the mattress. The ransack didn't take long and the person left without taking anything.

I huffed out a breath as I released the rewind to exclaim, "Whoever did this warded themselves from being seen."

His grim expression showed he'd already come to that conclusion. "Making this is an irregular robbery."

"As opposed to a regular one?" My sarcastic reply.

"I meant that this wasn't done to steal from me but because the person sought something."

"Something most likely related to our case."

"Maybe. We can't assume everything has to do with the chimera," he cautioned.

"What else then?"

"I don't know. I'm just saying we have to keep our minds open to all possibilities."

"In that case, let's see if anyone else got ransacked," I suggested. We knocked on a few doors. Some had occupants that shook their heads when asked if they'd had their rooms tampered with. Other rooms didn't reply when we knocked so I magicked the locks for a peek inside. No one else appeared to have been touched.

"Think they rifled through my place too?" Suddenly I had to wonder if my privacy had been violated. If it had, it would kind of confirm it had to do with the chimera because why else hit us both?

"Guess we'll soon find out."

As it turned out, I had worse than a home invasion to deal with. We arrived to find my place condemned.

My house leaned at an angle that promised imminent collapse, most likely due to the massive sinkhole in my driveway. Caution tape surrounded my property with a do-not-trespass message.

A pair of cop cars with flashing lights but no sirens sat outside. The cops most likely had been given the job of ensuring no one crossed into the danger zone.

I headed for the cop closest to me to ask, "What's going on?"

"Please stay behind the line, ma'am," the young human dared to say.

"I'm not crossing your bloody line, but I'd like to know what happened to my house!" I pointed.

"Water pipe burst. Caused part of the ground to

sink and shifted your foundation, rendering the structure unstable." A flat reply by the officer.

"I'm going to need to go inside and grab a few things."

"No."

"You can't be serious," I huffed. "I'm a CA agent."

"Sorry, ma'am. It's been deemed too dangerous. You'll want to call your insurance to start a claim."

I never asked for it, but I appreciated the arm Koda slid around my shoulders. A good thing he held me upright, as I lacked the strength to do so myself.

More than a decade of my life I'd spent in that house. I'd bought it on my own. Fixed it with the help of videos and home repair forums. It held all my worldly possessions, and I couldn't even go inside to get anything.

It hit me hard. The only good thing? My car remained at the CA office and not in the partially collapsed driveway. At least I'd have my vehicle to live in while I figured shit out. Who knew what my insurance would say. I had no idea if house collapse was covered.

"We should get going," I managed to say with a stiff upper lip. Don't get me wrong, it wanted to wobble like a Jell-O tower cake, but I refused to show how much this affected me.

"Agreed. We'll grab some takeout before heading back to Lenora's."

I glanced at him. "We're supposed to be going to the office."

"I somehow doubt you're in the mood to work."

"Someone fucked with my house." Before he could open his mouth, I added, "There's traces of magic seeping up from the ground. This was done intentionally, and that can only mean someone is upset with our investigation."

"Guess both our places getting hit is more than a coincidence at this point."

"Ya think?" I drawled. "Maybe you require more convincing."

"I'm just wondering what they thought we found that warranted this kind of measure."

"I don't know, but I think it's a sign we're getting close to getting a break in this case."

"Are we?"

"No idea, but I think at this point we need to pretend we do. Let's hit the CA office and flaunt. We'll tell anyone listening that we're getting close to catching the chimera. See if we can't draw the fucker who did this out in the open. Make them come after us."

"Chances are they won't attack if we're together."

"Agreed, which is why you and I are going to split up when we leave the office. One of us is sure to be followed. Once we figure out who has the tail, we'll activate a signal."

"What kind of signal?"

"The magical kind. Don't worry. I'll handle it. It's an easy spell to cast. Once the signal is activated, the other person will hightail it to act as backup."

"What if they're too far or too slow?"

"As you said before, we're both trained agents. We should be able to handle it."

"I'm not sure I like this plan," he stated as our ride share slid to a stop at the curb by the precinct.

"We can hash it out more at brunch because I don't know about you, but I need food."

We headed for the shop across the street from the CA. I used my partially-replenished magic to create a silence bubble around us so people wouldn't overhear, and then over pastries, hashbrowns, and sausages—the skinny breakfast kind and not his rather long and plump version—we discussed the plan. He would head for his hotel from the precinct before me. If he caught anyone following, he'd squeeze the ketchup packet I hexed to act as a beacon. I'd then go booking it to the rescue. If he wasn't followed, then he'd backtrack and pick up my trail as I took a circuitous route back to Lenora's. I had a spelled sugar packet tucked in my bra that would act as a tracker because, as Koda argued, *"What if they toss you in a van and drive you somewhere I can't track?"*

A valid point.

Once we finished breakfast, we split up. Him to head over to the precinct and get started, while I went shopping on the same block because I needed fresh clothes. He wasn't the only one who didn't want to be dragging an ass into the office wearing bedraggled garments. No need to get the rumor mill going, especially since there was nothing to tell—and not for lack of wanting.

When I entered the bull pen an hour later, no surprise, Koda had an entourage around his desk. I might have snuck off into a corner to do my own thing, but Kowalski signaled me from across the room.

I entered his office and shut the door, chirping. "What's up, boss?"

"I heard about your house. Are you okay?" His craggy features creased with concern.

"Yeah. I wasn't there when it happened." I grimaced. "They won't even let me inside to grab some stuff."

His lips pinched. "They don't want to be sued if something happens while you're in there, but I can probably pull a few strings and get some folks in there to pack up as much as they can."

"Really?" My expression brightened. "That'd be awesome."

"I just need to know where to deliver it. Do you have a place to stay?"

Almost I mentioned Lenora's, but to be honest, that seemed presumptuous. A few nights was one thing. Me moving in until I found a new place? That might be more than the banshee wanted.

"I think I'll have to rely on a storage place until I figure things out."

"If you need to, I have a spare room. Three actually. Always hoped I'd one day marry the woman of my dreams and have a family."

The offer to stay at his place surprised. "Thanks, but I'll probably just rent a motel room. The place off the highway offers a monthly option, and hey, it comes with weekly maid service."

"I'll understand if you need to take a leave of absence. Just bring me up to date on what you've discovered and then take all the time you need."

"No point in taking time off. What would I do? I'd rather keep working."

"Excellent." Kowalski's acceptance took me off-guard. "So you're making progress? I got your message about the fires last night and I sent the details along to the CA expert with a request for them to confirm chimera essence in the area."

"We have learned more. While we won't know until we hear back from your expert if all the fires are connected, my research shows that there does seem to be a path headed in our direction. However, I've discovered that they, including the four listed in the case file, are not in fact chimera-caused."

"Oh." His flat voice gave me no indication of his thoughts. "What makes you say that?"

"Color of the flames. Turns out chimera fires burn blue. But these, including the one that took out the cell phone store? Purple," I stated.

"Interesting. I didn't know that. About the color of the flames that is."

"Me either. Apparently, it's no longer common knowledge. Good thing I know someone who's a bit of a history buff."

"Who?"

Given the new boss might not be familiar with Lenora I didn't want to rat her out so I offered a vague, "Special informant whom I promised to keep under wraps." The boss didn't push the issue.

"How is it going with Koda? You are still working together, right?"

"Yeah. He's okay." Understatement. The man totally revved my engine, but that wasn't exactly the thing to tell your boss. "He's digging deepr into the purple fires."

"Why purple if she burns blue?"

"Because we think she's being followed. We're hoping that the locations that are being torched will give us a clue as to her intent."

"What does her intent matter? She's our escaped prisoner. A killer."

"Is she? Thus far, there don't seem to be any bodies attributed to her."

"She's dangerous," Kowalski insisted.

"If you say so. Makes me wonder if you got to see more of the redacted file than we did."

Rather than confirm, the boss replied, "Don't forget what I told you about their kind. They're tricksters, and they're responsible for unimaginable atrocities. Be on your guard. Don't engage. Call for backup."

"Assuming we find her. Thus far it's been a lot of dead ends. The one thing I did find out is she appears to have a bright blue eye that matches her hair and a dark one."

"Yeah, Whiteclaw told me you got a partial image from the clerk's memory. Can you bring it up for me now?"

"It's been too long, sorry." I could only recall someone else's memory for a short while without touching them again. "Shame the video got lost."

"We've got our best working to locate it," Kowalski declared. "Now, I guess I should let you get to work. Are you sticking around the office for a bit?"

"Most likely, unless something pops up. If we're lucky, my new partner will get a hit on some of those fires that we can check out."

I left my boss' office for the bull pen. Koda still held court with a handful of agents, mostly female I should add, which had me gnashing my teeth.

I headed up a floor to talk to Martha in requisitions about a new phone. I dreaded having to explain that, yes, I'd once again lost one. The reason for replacement box I had to fill in would be interesting. *Gargoyles have it.*

After that groveling, I headed to the rooftop, a favorite spot of mine when I needed to do some quiet thinking while still at the office. It annoyed me that our case had become so muddled. On the one hand, yes, the chimera was a fugitive who needed to be apprehended. On the other, something didn't sit right. If she was so dangerous, why hadn't we received any reports of her terrorizing towns and civilians? Why did the fires burn purple, not blue? And why did she appear to be heading in this direction?

I really wished I still had the redacted file, as I'd been wondering if I could use magic to decipher it. Alas, the file remained in the secret library. Would the gargoyles have gone back to sleep yet? Would they let me pop in to grab my satchel with my stuff? Only one way to find out. Problem being, go alone or drag along my new partner?

I headed down to the bullpen to see if I could steal Koda, only Chrissie, of the petite blonde perky tits and bright smile, sat on his desk, making sure she giggled often. I'd love to have hated her, only she really was a sweet woman, if a flirt.

Since he seemed busy, and I found myself annoyed, I snuck out through the CA basement. Foolish? Not in my mind since I never technically left the building, which, in turn, meant no one would know to follow. The basement had an entrance to the sewer, which, after two wrong turns, let me exit close to the church. Then it was a simple matter of making my way to the library. I made it without mishap, and I halted my steps in shock as I noticed the stairs to the book trove already down and the hatch entrance open.

Was someone inside? I'd never come across anyone before. Technically, anyone could have access, especially considering that even Lenora had known about it in her time.

I went up the steps cautiously, and as my head crested the threshold, I gasped.

The library had been destroyed. By fire and by force.

While the stone structure itself remained intact, the books and shelves had been reduced to ash and darkened bits. The gargoyle protectors smashed to pieces. Like Humpty, they couldn't be put back together again.

Through the rubble, I spotted a familiar shape. No surprise, my satchel hadn't survived, although, a poke of it showed the leather exterior had somewhat protected its insides. My leather wallet had survived, but as for the rest of it? Melted plastic was all that was left of my phone, and ashes for the files.

I felt a pang for losing them both. There wouldn't be a chance to try to get more information from the redacted chimera files... and there wouldn't be a chance for me to look further into my own history.

As I surveyed the destroyed room, I once more cast a rewind spell to see what happened.

It didn't surprise me to see the same blurry figure of before, arms raised, casting magic that blasted the gargoyles then ignited the dry books with purple flames. Was this the same person who'd gone through Koda's room? Much like his space, they didn't appear to take anything. Never even went a step past the hatch. Their sole purpose appeared to be to destroy.

Which could only mean they feared something in this room.

Just before they turned to leave, a haze blurred everything, not that it mattered at that point. I'd seen enough.

As the mirage faded, I got smacked by a sudden fear.

Koda's hotel had been ransacked, my home and the library destroyed. All places I'd visited in search of information. While the first two locations would be common knowledge, the last should have been a secret, yet somehow the blurry assailant knew to come here. What did that mean for Lenora's home?

Suddenly panicked. I fled the underground tunnels, taking only a second to fire off a text to Koda telling him where I was going. Since I lost phones so often, I always kept the cloud backup option on so my new phones would immediately have all the information from the old, including my contacts.

I had a taxi drop me off just outside the abandoned blocks of buildings surrounding Lenora's place.

I huffed as I walked, my pace rapid enough to give me shin splints. When her intact house came into sight, I sighed in relief but didn't slow my gait. I knocked and entered, shouting, "Lenora! Where are you? Lenora!"

"Goodness. What's with the bellowing?" She floated down the stairwell from the second floor.

My relief had me sagging. "There you are. I was worried about you."

"Whatever for?" she trilled.

"Because I might have dragged you into danger. We need to relocate you somewhere safer."

"Safer than here?" Lenora scoffed.

"It's no longer safe. I made a mistake in staying

with you, as it appears my current investigation has drawn attention. The bad kind. An unknown assailant destroyed my home last night. Tore through Koda's room. Even torched the gargoyle library."

Her face took on a sly expression. "And you think they would dare to do the same here?"

"I don't know, but I didn't want to take a chance. Now I'm just hoping in my haste I didn't accidentally lead them here."

"Let them come. They'll see I'm not easily intimidated."

"Oh, Lenora," I sighed. The banshee in her craved the excitement of a battle, but the reality might not be what she hoped for.

My new cell phone rang, the SIM card transferring over my old number keeping me accessible to those with my contact. The call display said Whiteclaw, so I answered. "Hello, partner."

"Don't you hello me. Where the fuck are you?" his tight query.

"I texted you. I'm at Lenora's."

"Without me?" he hissed. "We had a plan."

"Something came up."

"That prevented you from calling? We're supposed to be a team."

"Sorry."

"I highly doubt that," his dry reply.

"If it helps, I'm fine, but the library isn't. The same person who rifled through your room set it on fire and destroyed the gargoyles."

He uttered a low whistle. "Well, shit. Guess that explains why you went haring off to Lenora's. I take it she's fine?"

"Yes."

"Good. Stay there and wait for me. I might have found something."

"Oh? What?"

"I'd rather not say over the phone. I'm heading over."

"Take my car. There's a spare keyset in a magnetic box in the rear passenger wheel well."

"On my way. Sit tight. Don't go anywhere and be careful."

Good advice, only it came a tad too late.

The moment I hung up, Lenora stiffened. Even her hair stopped undulating as she whispered, "Something evil this way comes."

CHAPTER 9

Koda wanted to curse. He'd been so caught up in his research, while also trying to spot who might be a mole, he never noticed when Marissa left Abe's office. He assumed she'd remained in the building. Wrong. The woman had taken off to go who knew where, by herself, he might add, without a word to him.

He'd only realized she had a phone when, in his search for her at the precinct, he discovered she'd been to requisition and assigned a new cell.

So he'd called and she'd answered with the gall to warn him to be careful. He wasn't the one who'd hared off on his own, ignoring their plan. The urge to yell filled him. He wanted to shake her for being so foolish. Then kiss her for scaring him.

Yes, kiss. He'd not been able to stop thinking of her. Imagining her naked body. The press of her lips against his.

She'd tried to seduce him, and he'd blown her off.

Why, exactly? Fear for starters. He feared what sex between them might mean. He'd never been one to believe in the whole love at first sight, or when it came to those who shifted skin, the mating instinct, yet no denying something about her drew him like no other.

Then there was the distraction factor. If they got involved, he might pay more attention to her than the mission, which, admittedly, had already occurred. She consumed his thoughts and made him rash.

Look at him, exiting the precinct without a care, not even checking for a shadow. He found the car keys where she'd mentioned and soon hit the road, juggling his phone as he attempted to map where he had to go.

As he headed in her direction, his phone rang. Marissa called. Probably to ask him to bring food.

"What's up?"

"They found us."

No need to ask which they.

His blood turned cold as he replied, "Can you hold off long enough for me to get there?"

"I don't know. I'm not even sure what we're facing. Lenora keeps repeating evil is coming."

"Get to the second floor and barricade yourself in a room. I'll be there as fast as I can."

"I think I'm going to have to fight. I hear glass breaking in the front."

In the background, Lenora screeched, "How dare you invade my house!"

He floored the gas pedal. "I'm still at least ten minutes away."

"I don't think they're going to wait for you to arrive. I gotta go." She hung up before he could—

Could what? Yell at her to keep him on the line? She had to fight, not reassure him. Right now, the only thing he could do? Get there faster.

As if to mock his urgency, a loud pop preceded a tire blowing out. The car wobbled and swerved before he braked to a stop. He exited to glare at the offending rubber with its giant hole.

"Unfucking real," he muttered. He didn't have time to change the tire. Nor would he make it fast enough on foot. Not two feet at any rate.

Time to flip into an animal shape. Unlike werewolves, he didn't have to strip, nor did he lose the things he wore. As a skinwalker, his magic transformed him as he was, preserving his clothing and anything else he carried. In this case, a snowy white owl with mighty wings, one of his favorite shapes. He lifted into the air, flapping hard to get above the buildings, and then made a beeline for Lenora's house. He didn't need a GPS or directions. Instinct guided him, and air currents caught his extended wings. What would have been ten minutes by car took a mere fraction of the time.

And even then, he arrived seemingly too late.

Smoke billowed from the house. Purple flames jetted from blown-out windows. He coasted downward, not into the front yard but the back where he could see movement, namely a pair of big black dogs dragging a limp Marissa from the house.

With a scree of challenge, he dove, ready to claw out the eyes of the dogs, only to pull up short as an agitated Lenora slung herself in front of him.

The banshee weaved back and forth, wailing. "My home. My babies. My home. My memories. My home." The shrill tone of her lament grated but could be tolerated. The dogs standing guard on either side of Marissa, though? That he needed to handle.

It reassured to see they weren't trying to eat her; however, given they were strangers, he didn't trust. He landed and flipped to his human skin, fully dressed and very annoyed.

"Move away from the woman," he commanded.

The dog on the left cocked its head and lolled its tongue.

"Don't make me hurt you," he threatened. The owl was only one of the animals he could call.

The canine on the right yipped and, he'd have sworn, smirked.

Lenora dipped low enough to show him her crazed eyes as she clasped her hands, moaning, "I've lost everything."

He had no reply to that because she actually had. First her family and then her only link to them. With no home, where would a sad banshee live?

"What's wrong with Marissa?" He used the question to try and snap Lenora out of her shock.

"Gas. They gassed the house and knocked her out. But it didn't work on me! The coward, though, didn't come inside. Oh no. The evil one stayed out there, weaving wicked magic. Lighting a fire to flush us out."

"What's with the dogs?" Koda asked.

"I don't know. They smashed through the kitchen door and dragged Marissa outside before the flames could consume her flesh."

"Where is the attacker?" Because he'd not seen anyone else on his descent.

"Gone. The coward didn't stay to face me." Lenora grimaced. "A pity. I would have made the evil one's ears bleed with the things I had to say."

"Keep an eye out for more trouble while I check on Marissa." He approached her prone body slowly. Even so, the dogs growled at him. Not in the mood, he growled right back. "Move out of the way, furballs. I'm trying to help her."

To his surprise, they shifted away from her and kept a wary watch. He'd already figured out they acted as friend, not foe. Still, Koda remained cautious as he knelt by Marissa's unconscious body, concerned by her slow-rising chest and shallow breaths. Alive, but the gas Lenora mentioned had knocked her out. For how long? No idea. She appeared unharmed, at least. Still, he couldn't have her asleep, not when danger might still lurk.

Despite how it looked, he knew of only one way to wake her. He dipped his head and pressed his mouth to hers, murmuring a chant he'd learned at a shaman's knee, one to share vitality.

As his strength siphoned into her, her breathing

deepened, her lips softened and parted against his. A tiny moan escaped as she turned his embrace to revive into one to excite. He leaned away, the shock of it enough that she gasped and sat bolt upright, eyes wide and yet unseeing.

"Marissa." He crooned her named softly.

Her head pivoted. "Koda?" Her brow creased. "What happened? Why do I smell smoke?" As she asked, her head tilted and she gaped at the raging inferno.

"Lenora's fine," he stated before being asked.

"No, I'm not," wailed the banshee. "It's all gone. I have nothing. NOTH-INGGGG!"

The treble in those last syllables caused him to grunt and clasp his hands over his ears. Marissa also winced.

"Help me up." She held out her hand to him, and he hauled her to her feet. Only when she wobbled upright did she notice the dogs. "Where did they come from?"

"No idea, but they saved your life," his begrudging reply, barely heard over the banshee's caterwauling.

"We have to do something about Lenora," Marissa grimly stated.

"Like what? Because usually there's only one real option for a banshee who's lost control."

"I'm aware," she grumbled.

"What usually calms her?"

"The last time she got agitated I managed to play some rewind memories of her children chasing each other in the house and baking cookies with her. They left an imprint in the rooms that I could tap."

Given the billowing black smoke spewing from the house, that didn't seem like an option.

A glance at the yard gave Koda an idea. "What about reviving those past moments out here?"

Her lips pursed. "I told you before, it works best within walls."

"It's worth a shot."

"I don't even know if they were out here much."

"They were kids. Kids play outside." Especially forty years ago.

"I guess it doesn't hurt to try."

She wavered on her feet, and he steadied her. "Maybe we should wait. You're still shaking off the effects of the gas."

"I have to do something. Lenora's about to snap."

Indeed, her chanting had changed to, "Took my babies. Kill them. Burned my babies. Kill them."

"How can I help?"

"How about another kiss?" Her lips quirked.

"Um."

She chuckled. "How about later, then. First, let's see if we can't calm Lenora down." Marissa held out her hands and closed her eyes. She murmured, "There is something here. But it's faint." Her expression creased as she strained, and he moved behind her to offer support.

To his surprise, the big dogs tucked in other either side, and she dug her fingers into their fur, exhaling as she did. "They're feeding me magic," she exclaimed, sounding stronger.

Before he could ask her to explain what she meant, the yard shifted. The tree that loomed had a much shorter ghostly version. The bushes flowered. A pair of children, a girl and a boy, ran with a net, chasing a butterfly.

"My babies." The whisper brought Lenora to drift close to the reenactment. A single tear tracked down her cheek.

"Mama, Mama, come and play with us," chirped the little girl with bobbing pigtails.

"I want to, baby girl." Lenora reached out, the longing in her clear.

Marissa stiffened before muttering, "Something's happening."

"What do you mean?" he replied.

"My magic..." She grunted.

"Shut it off."

"I can't," she gasped.

The boy's ghostly figure stared straight at Lenora. "We miss you, Mama."

"I miss you too," Lenora cried as big fat tears rolled down her cheeks.

"It's time," the girl stated.

"I want to go," Lenora wailed. "But I'm afraid. What if I can't find you?"

"We'll guide you, Mama." The little girl and boy walked to Lenora and reached out their hands. Lenora gripped them both tight. It should have been impossible.

For one, it was supposed to be a memory, which shouldn't have been interactive. Two, ghosts had no substance. Given that, plus Marissa's trembling and the cold oozing from her frame, he had a feeling strong magic worked through her.

"Come, Mama." The children urged Lenora to walk with them.

"Where are we going?" she asked, following without hesitation.

"To be a family. Papa is waiting." As the boy spoke, a bright fissure appeared, a doorway made of light and in it, the silhouette of a man.

"Bernard." Lenora exhaled a name, and the children giggled.

The girl lisped, "Mama's gonna kiss him again."

"Ew!" exclaimed the boy.

Indeed, once Lenora reached the door, the man took her into his arms and held her tight as he gave her a long lingering embrace.

"Quick, Mama. We have to get inside before the door closes." The girl and boy tugged at her, but Lenora needed no urging. With her ghost husband's arm around her waist, she walked into the light.

Once it blinked out, Marissa collapsed into Koda's arms.

CHAPTER 10

The flames danced all around, pretty lights that I reached out to grab, only they slipped through my fingers. I didn't fear the fire, but I didn't like being alone.

"Mama?" I called for her, but she didn't reply. I thought about going to look, but she'd told me to hide. Hide because the bad man found us.

What bad man?

Forget. Forget. Forget. As the fire consumed the house around me, so, too, did it take my thoughts. My memories. It burned everything away...

I roused from my slumber brought on by exhaustion in a bed I didn't recognize, flanked by big black dogs. The same ones that pulled me from the fire at Lenora's house.

Thinking of the banshee caused a pang. Poor Lenora had moved on, leaving this world for the next, reunited finally with the family she missed so much, and hopefully at peace. I just wished I hadn't been the reason for her permanent death, even if it had a good outcome.

The house had been attacked because of me.

Lenora had flitted around muttering, "If evil thinks it can come inside, I'll show it. This is my house."

"What do you mean by evil?" I asked.

"Can't you feel it? The menace that oozes." Lenora glanced at the bay window and murmured, "He is consumed with hatred."

He, so, not the chimera then. I wondered if it was the person who'd wrecked my house. If so, I had a score to settle.

Not being suicidal, I called Koda, even as I knew he'd never make it in time. Sure enough, the attack came while we spoke.

Crash. The window broke as something impacted it, the object hitting the floor and rolling to land a few paces from my feet. I cast a shield the moment I heard the crack, a shield to prevent being hit by shrapnel or an explosive force. It did nothing to stop the gas that suddenly oozed from the canister, filling the air too quickly for me to escape.

The thick, cloying gas knocked me out. Next thing I recalled, Koda kissed me. A nice way to regain consciousness. It reminded me of a fairy tale where the prince woke his princess.

It didn't last long enough. The moment he realized I'd woken, he pulled away. I'd then proceeded to overdo it casting a memory spell in hopes of calming Lenora, and *poof*. I woke in a strange bed with even stranger dogs. Dogs that had boosted my magic in Lenora's yard.

Or so it seemed at the time.

Out of curiosity, I stroked my fingers through the sleek black fur and held in a gasp as the light touch bumped up my magical strength.

It felt like Hekate, and I suddenly remembered my goddess' favor for canines. "Did she send you?" I wondered aloud.

The dog I stroked rolled to his back and lolled his tongue. I'd take that as a yes.

The door to the room swung open, and Koda walked in, carrying a large tray. Upon seeing me, he exclaimed, "Good, you're awake. I had a feeling you might be. I brought you some sustenance." He lowered the platter, on which balanced a glass of orange juice, a steaming mug of what better be coffee, and a plate of food. A big plate, I should add, piled with pastries, fruit, and bacon.

"Mmm." I pushed to a seated position, my mouth watering. I needed to refuel more than just my magic.

Koda eyed the dogs pressed to either side of me. "Time for you furballs to get down so she can eat."

The one on my left offered Koda a lazy eye before slinking off the bed. His canine twin followed, leaving Koda a spot to settle the tray.

"Where are we?" I asked as I reached for the juice. I wanted to take care of my pasty tongue first.

"Abe's house."

I almost spat out my mouthful of orange juice. I managed a hard swallow before saying, "You brought me to the boss's place?"

"With Lenora's place burned to the ground, and your house condemned, I had no idea where else to go."

"A hotel would have worked."

"The last one got ransacked, and so I wanted something a little more secure."

I crunched a piece of bacon before I replied. "I can't stay here." Kowalksi didn't deserve to have his house torched for harboring me. "Whoever is starting the fires followed me to the gargoyle library and to Lenora's. They'll come here next."

"There was no sign of anyone around Lenora's house. Abe had a team look everywhere and they found no sign of the chimera or someone else who might be starting fires. Just to be safe, they cloaked you and the dogs when we took you out so no one saw. Whoever started that fire thinks you're dead."

"You're assuming no one on that team is crooked."

"If they are, you really think they're going to blow their cover by attacking their boss's house?"

"I suppose not." The logic did make sense. "Where is Abe? Is he here?"

"No, he's back at the precinct leading the investigation into your attempted murder."

"Damn." I never thought I'd hear a sentence that included me and attempted murder.

"Now that you're awake, we can decide our next move."

I snorted. "What move? We still don't have the slightest idea what's going on."

"Not so quick. I found something while looking into the fires yesterday."

That piqued my interest. I held off on biting my pastry and asked, "You going to spill or make me beg?"

"As if you'd beg."

"Why, Koda, are you hoping I'll get on my knees for some oral groveling?"

He blinked. His cheeks turned a ruddy color, and I'll bet if I looked lower, he'd have a hard-on.

One of the dogs chuffed, as if it understood.

I munched on my pastry as Koda collected himself.

He cleared his throat. "Since we know so little about the chimera, I decided to do some digging into the past, specifically around the time she was arrested, to see if we could find any patterns that match what we are seeing now. I started by looking at fires reported to be magic-caused rather than naturally occurring. Of them, I found two reported to have blue flames."

My interest heightened even further. I'd almost started to wonder if Lenora had been wrong about blue fire, since we'd not found any evidence to suggest it existed. "Go on. Don't keep me in suspense, unless you want to tease me. I should warn, I can be impatient. You might have to tie me down." I couldn't stop the innuendo, mostly because it was so fun to put him off-kilter.

It took him a second to compose himself. He cleared his throat. "The first blue-flamed fire occurred in a hospital records room, thirty-six years ago."

"And the second?"

"The next happened in this town about six years later in an abandoned house."

At the mention, my blood froze. I immediately thought of the report I'd uncovered about myself. I tried to shake it away, but my brain did the math. *If the hospital fire was thirty-six years ago, and the house fire was six years later, that means the house fire was thirty years ago, which is exactly the same years ago as when I was found in the ashes of a burned-down house.*

Surely a coincidence. House fires weren't an uncommon occurrence. Besides, the report I'd recovered about me didn't mention blue flames, at least not in the pages I'd been able to read. Not surprising, though, since I knew those writing reports often neglected minor, to them, details.

Given Koda waited for my reply, I had to blurt out something. "Are these two fires the reasons she was locked up?" Two fires didn't seem to account for "crimes against humanity" to the degree we'd been led to believe, and it also didn't explain why her file had been redacted to the extreme, but maybe it was a start.

"I don't know. But they're not enough to warrant an incarceration of thirty-plus years since neither of those fires had casualties."

"Meaning there's more we to discover." I munched on another piece of bacon as my brain processed and I tried not to let it show that I was freaking out a little bit.

"That or the other fires *had* been done by her.

Maybe the chimera found a way to change the color of her fire."

I sipped at my coffee before thinking out loud. "The two local purple fires were at a motel and an abandoned mall, but I didn't have time to look into the other dozen from the past six months. Do you have my phone?"

As I asked, I saw it on the nightstand, plugged into a charger. Koda handed it to me before I could reach, and I quickly opened my email. I'd copied myself in on the message I'd sent Abe so I'd have all the information to look at later.

"So, where were they?" Koda asked after giving me a moment to read.

"Some seem like random locations, but others, not so much. The first purple-flamed arson hit a Cryptid Authority storage facility for older cases. Then there was one at a CA science lab. Another, took out a government foster agency office. There's also a school." The more I read, the more my blood chilled.

"What is it?" he asked.

"The school..." I felt faint, and my hand trembled.

"What's got you looking pale?"

"The school is Trinity of the Three. I went there." I hated how shaky my voice sounded, but I'd never had a case hitting so close to home before.

"Probably a coincidence."

"I didn't believe in those."

There was one more attachment with details of a residential fire, but I didn't want to open it yet. I just couldn't. Instead, I told Koda, "I need the address of the house that burned down, the one from thirty years ago."

My churning stomach had a feeling I knew what we'd discover about both addresses.

Thirty-six years ago a hospital records room burned. Meanwhile, I didn't know where I'd been born, nor my date of birth. When I'd been found, since the children's services lacked an identity, they assigned me a generic last name, Smith, and fabricated a birth certificate using the date of the fire as the day of my birth, and the age I claimed for the year.

I recalled being asked, *How old are you?* and holding up all my fingers on one hand, but what does a kid know? I could have easily been six. I'm sure plenty of children forget to add a finger to their claimed age after a recent birthday. Kids didn't always know or care about the finer details.

Rather than ask why my interest in the address, Koda gave me a curt nod. "Give me a second, and I'll see if I can get someone in the office to send me a pic of the notes I took. When I left the precinct, I kind of did so in haste and left them on my desk."

"Why, Koda, be careful, or I'll start to think you care."

"Too late," he grumbled before he left the room. Pity he couldn't take my trepidation with him.

My agitation meant I couldn't stay in bed. I swung my legs off the edge, opposite the tray of food. As my feet hit the floor, I stood and regretted it. Dizzy spots danced in front of my eyes, and weakness plagued my limbs. I felt myself falling, only someone caught me!

Surprised, since I knew Koda hadn't returned yet, I found myself gaping into the face of a very handsome man. His skin a burnished ebony, his hair cut short, his eyes a vivid blue.

"Who are you? Where did you come from?" I huffed just as a man with light skin but dark hair and matching blue eyes stood behind him.

"Hekate sent us," the dark-skinned guy replied in a low tone.

It took me a second to make the connection. "You're the dogs!"

"We are," said the second fellow.

"Why did Hekate send you?" A surprise since my goddess had been even quieter than usual of late.

"She thought you could use help, and since she's busy and we were bored..." The man with the light skin grinned. "Who wouldn't bark at the chance to help an attractive witch?"

"Unhand her!" Koda's sudden roar had me whipping my head. My partner had returned and appeared ready to attack. I might be a strong independent woman, but I'll admit a part of me enjoyed his macho reaction. Still, that didn't mean I could let the hounds be hurt.

"It's okay. They're here because of Hekate."

"They're naked," Koda growled, a fact I'd not noticed until he pointed it out.

And of course, then I just had to look. Muscles.

Abs. Limp dicks. Impressive in repose but nothing like Koda's. That man could have given them penis envy. "They shifted. Of course they're nude," I replied, trying to defuse the situation.

"They should have found some clothing first before sexually harassing you." Koda continued to glare.

"I'm sure they would have if they'd had time."

"She almost fainted," added the one who'd not caught me.

Immediately, Koda's concern turned to me. "Are you okay? Do you need to get back in bed?"

"I'm fine. Just a little lightheaded from the exertion. That spell I used in Lenora's yard kicked my ass." My explanation didn't stop Koda from sliding close to me, ready to be my chivalrous knight should I stumble again. What did it say about me that it tempted me to swoon on purpose?

"That was some epic spellcasting," said the shifter who'd caught me. "Hekate mentioned you were strong, but damn."

"Who are you that you're so familiar with a goddess?" Koda questioned.

"According to the history texts, we're her personal pets," joked the fair-skinned guy. "Which is insulting. We're her scions, tasked with acting on her behalf."

"What's your names?" I asked.

"I'm Orion," spoken with a bow by the more jovial of the pair. "And this grumpy dog is Ambrose."

"I am not grumpy," grumped Ambrose. "I just happen to take our work seriously."

"How is it I'm only finding out you're shapeshifters now? If I'd known, I would have never left you alone with Marissa." Koda still appeared pissed.

"You never asked." Ambrose shrugged with his reply.

"And your witch was perfectly safe. The goddess sent us to protect her. A good thing too, or she'd have been barbecued."

A reminder that only pinched Koda's lips further. "Go find some clothes," he snapped.

"Jeezus, for a skinwalker, you're awfully prudish," grumbled Ambrose as he stalked out of the room with a nicely flexing ass.

Orion took a moment to say, "We're not interested in your woman, so you can relax," before he left.

The comment raised my brow. "Your woman?"

Koda's jaw tensed. "Don't know what they're talking about."

"Says the man having a jealous fit," I pointed out.

"Not jealous," he mumbled.

"Then maybe I should call them back in," I teased, to which I received a glare. My lips quirked. "It's okay if you like me. I like you, too. And that kiss... I wouldn't mind another one of those."

"That can't happen. We have a job to do."

"And you think us having sex would affect it?"

"Yes."

My smile widened. "I'm flattered you think I'm

that good, but here's a different perspective. Our ignoring our needs might be more distracting."

"How so?"

"Well, for one, I might not be listening for danger, if I'm too busy masturbating."

His jaw dropped, and he appeared speechless.

Me, I had more to say. "Really, if we want us to be at our best, then we should be fucking to get it out of our system."

"That's crude."

"But honest," I added. "Here's the thing. I find you good-looking. Very much so as a matter of fact, and I think you're attracted to me as well."

"Understatement," he muttered under his breath.

"So we're both hot for each other. We're also both adults with a strong sense of responsibility, meaning we're capable of having sex without any of the emotional drama."

"Are you seriously advocating for us to become lovers?"

Was I? "Would that really be so bad?"

He raked fingers through his hair as he sighed, "No."

"Maybe once you get a taste of me, you'll lose the jealousy."

"Doubtful," his dry reply.

"I didn't take you for the possessive type." And I liked it more than I'd have imagined.

"That's just it, I'm not. But there's something

about you…" He shook his head. "I can't believe we're having this conversation."

Me neither, and yet it felt liberating. Especially since when I moved close to him, he didn't retreat but rather placed his hands on my hips, drawing me nearer.

I tilted my head and pursed my lips. "Kiss me."

"You're still recovering," he reminded.

"The ache I've got isn't from an injury," I teased.

His nostrils flared. "Now might not be the time. We're not alone."

"I don't see anyone else in the room, do you?" I draped my arms around his neck.

"You make it hard to say no."

"Then don't," I whispered, leaning as high as I could, but it took him bending to meet me before I could touch his lips.

His groan of surrender made me quiver, but his kiss melted me.

CHAPTER 11

OF ALL THE THINGS KODA SHOULD BE DOING, KISSING Marissa shouldn't have made the list. Yet once his mouth touched hers, he wanted nothing else.

She made a good point about his desire for her being a distraction. However, he feared that rather than slake his thirst, one taste and he'd become addicted.

Actually, he knew once wouldn't be enough.

And he no longer cared.

He wanted her, and right now that was all that mattered. His mouth pressed firmly against hers, and she replied by parting her lips, the tip of her tongue teasing. As if that sensual delight weren't enough, she gripped his shoulders, held herself close, the press of her body a titillating delight even with their clothes on.

She had to crane to keep their lips locked, and even then, he had to lean to meet her. His hands cupped her sweet cheeks, using them to lift her higher, giving him better access to her mouth, which meant his tongue could play with hers. A sensual slide of flesh that went well with their already panting breath.

"Take off your shirt," she ordered, the words soft pants against his lips. Her fingers dug at the fabric, and he had to set her down to strip it off. As it cleared his head, he realized she'd removed her own top and stood there in only her bra.

So fucking sexy. He reached out and hooked a strap with a finger, dragging it off her shoulder. Then the other. He tugged the cups down to reveal her breasts, more beautiful than he remembered, the bright berries of them puckering at his regard.

He dragged her back for another kiss, his hands once more using her ass to lift. Her mouth hot and demanding on his. The hard tips of her nipples poking at his chest, a teasing friction that had him eager for a taste. But that would mean breaking off the kiss, and he wasn't ready for that.

Instead, he used his grip on her butt to grind her against him, to press his throbbing cock, confined still in his pants, against her.

Her breath caught, and she growled, "I think it's time we moved to the bed. And lose those pants."

He wasn't about to argue. His pants hit the floor a second before hers. She kept only her panties on as she crawled onto the bed. He just about lost it seeing the waggle of her ass.

When she flipped onto her back and beckoned, he

wasted no time joining her. His knees hit the mattress between her parted legs. He leaned over her, mesmerized by her sultry parted lips, the smoldering desire in her gaze.

She reached for Koda and dragged him down for a kiss that just about had him coming. He'd never been so aroused. So needy. He returned the kiss, devouring her mouth, his tongue hot and probing, his lips tugging and suckling, his pleasure emerging in a humming sound he couldn't stop.

When his lips slid from her lips to her ear, she gasped. "Ooh." A sound repeated when he sucked at the sensitive lobe.

He moved down her body, lips brushing the silky expanse of her neck then the curve of her collar bone. He rubbed his face in the valley of her breasts, and she writhed at his teasing touch, her fingers fisting the fabric of the comforter.

Her nipples pointed at attention, two perfect berries for plucking. He couldn't help but suck one.

"Oh." She arched under his caress. Grabbed his head and pushed him to take even more into his mouth. More than happy to comply, he teased her, alternating between her breasts, sucking the nipples, teasing them between his teeth until she writhed and mewled.

Only then did he move lower, his mouth skimming over her belly until he met the edge of her panties. He used only his teeth to tug them down, easing them past her hips and down her legs.

He couldn't help but stare. She didn't cross her legs or cover herself but rather slid a hand down her body and stroked the pink petals of her sex.

Sexiest damned thing ever.

He nestled himself between her legs and kissed the hand that stroked between her lips. Then lapped across her clit. She cried out, and her hand went from teasing to grabbing the comforter. With her all his to enjoy, he licked again and again. Teasing her button, spreading her soft petals that he might dip into the honey seeping from her sex. She tasted so sweet. He wanted nothing more than to make her come against his tongue.

He kept flicking at her clit but also inserted two fingers, hooking them to press against the inner wall of her sex, knowing he found her sweet spot by the way her hips bucked.

His free arm pinned her down, and he worked her. Sucked and lapped at her clit. Fingered her G-spot. Felt her tightening around him until she came hard, uttering a strident cry that made him swell with pleasure.

But he didn't stop. His tongue continued to flick rapidly, and his fingers kept thrusting until he felt her getting tight again. Only then did he rise to a kneeling position between her thighs.

She opened eyes heavy with desire and smiled in a way that made his heart stutter.

She reached for him, and he fell against her, their lips meeting in a passionate embrace while the tip of him pressed against her wet pussy. He slid in slowly and just about came at the tight fit of her.

Her fingers dug into his shoulders as she groaned into his mouth, "That feels incredible." Her hips wiggled, and he almost lost it.

"You're driving me insane," he grunted as he pushed deeper and she clenched.

"Good," her reply. She nipped his lower lip. "Now stop being so gentle and give it to me."

Her demand drew a heavy groan, but he also obeyed. His hips began to rock, the thickness of his cock snug inside her tight channel, and it suctioned at him as he pushed in and out. But her slick honey made the glide easy. He thrust. Slamming deep until she made a sound then pulling out enough to make her mewl.

His pumping strokes soon had her panting and digging her nails into him. She huffed too hard to kiss, but that was fine because he was doing his best to hold on. Not easy. Her channel squeezed and fisted his cock so tight that each stroke brought a deep shudder. But he couldn't come. Not until she came again.

He thrust faster, their bodies moving in a rhythm that had them both flushed and breathless.

When she came, her sex squeezed him so tight he couldn't hold back.

Didn't want to. He came so hard he left his body for a second.

He collapsed atop her, only for a moment before rolling them so she lay atop his chest.

Where she belonged.

She rested her head against his pec and said nothing. What could they say? Best sex ever? How about this might have been more than a one-time fling?

She's the one.

The problem being how to convince her of that. He had a hard time wrapping his own head around it.

"Well that was fun," she purred against him.

Fun? A transcendent experience and she called it fun!

He might have replied, but a knock at the door interrupted.

Ambrose hollered, "You guys want pizza?"

"Oh hell yeah. Food." Marissa rolled off him, and the intimacy ended.

But there would be another.

He'd make sure of it.

CHAPTER 12

As I chewed my slice of pizza, I kept calling myself dumb for opening my mouth and saying the wrong thing. How could I have called the most epic sex of my life fun? It had been so much more than that. However, I couldn't take the words back, and worse, I couldn't read Koda.

He'd dressed in silence after our interruption. No soft touches or looks, no playful banter. Was he insulted? Then again, I should know this was how people acted after no-strings sex. In the past, I'd gotten what I needed and gone on my merry way. But now, it left me perturbed.

I'll admit I'm not sure what I expected. A declaration of love would have had me snorting. I didn't need to be coddled. Never needed it before, didn't need it now, either. So why did I keep glancing at Koda waiting for him to... what? Treat me like his girlfriend? I'd been the one to recommend sex to reduce the tension between us. Never once did I advocate for something more. Then again, neither did he. What if he'd not been as impressed? What if I spoke up and it turned out he didn't feel the same way? Best I keep my mouth shut.

But what if keeping quiet meant it never happened again?

Ugh. No wonder I remained single.

While we ate, Koda questioned Hekate's hounds, who'd followed instructions and found themselves some clothing.

"Where do you live when you're not on a mission for your goddess?"

"We have an apartment in New York, but we don't see it much given the goddess has us moving about quite a bit in her name."

"Doing what?" I asked before taking a bite of gooey cheese with a crispy pepperoni. It surprised me to hear Hekate kept them busy, given she didn't much involve herself in the world these days.

Ambrose offered a vague reply. "A little bit of everything."

Orion added on to that. "If the goddess is being threatened, we work to circumvent. If a friend of hers needs aid, we provide it."

"You have magic," I stated. I still remembered the feel of it flowing into me from them when I cast the spell in Lenora's yard.

"We carry the goddess' blessing with us, but only those in her favor can use it."

"And she was the one to send you to Marissa?" Koda clarified.

"Yup. We would have arrived sooner but someone"—Ambrose turned a glare on Orion—"forgot to rent a car before we got on the plane."

"Well excuse me," Orion drawled. "How was I to know a convention in town would mean we'd have trouble finding transportation?"

"Did you see who attacked Marissa?" While Koda had a plate with a few slices, he didn't appear to be eating much.

Hekate's servants glanced at each other, and Orion shrugged. "Sorry. But no. We arrived in time to see the smoke starting to seep out of the house, and we charged in to see if anyone needed rescuing."

"Good thing too," Ambrose added. "The banshee wasn't exactly worried about the witch passed out on her living room floor."

My lips pursed. "Lenora had other things on her mind, such as the attack on her home, which was entirely my fault. I should have never involved her."

To my surprise, Koda leaned over and put his hand over mine. "You couldn't have known what would happen. And from the looks of it, you actually did Lenora a favor. You reunited her with her family."

True, but that didn't stop the sad tilt of my lips. "I hope she's at peace now."

Koda removed his hand from mine, only to place it on my leg, just above my knee. Possessive, without being overbearing. It gave me a tiny thrill. Maybe what I felt wasn't one-sided.

Orion had questions. "So am I getting this straight? You don't know who your enemy is?"

I sipped on a can of cola, swishing the bubbly sugared liquid around before I swallowed. "There's a few possibilities." It took us a few minutes to explain our current case, what we'd found thus far, and by the time we finished, even the jovial Orion frowned.

"Sounds complicated," he commented.

"Because there's a missing piece," Ambrose interjected. "There has to be something linking all these events, and I don't just mean the chimera."

Me. I hadn't yet voiced the suspicion that had been growing with each new detail we learned about the fires. I feared I'd sound like some kind of narcissist, making the case all about me. And yet...

"Speaking of pieces." Koda held out his phone and pointed at the screen. "I got that address."

I dreaded looking at the pictures of his notes, even as I needed to be sure. I stared at the neat handwriting, and my stomach clenched as my fear manifested.

A watching Koda saw the change in my expression. "What's wrong?"

I shook my head, unable to answer. Still hoping I was wrong and as though on auto-pilot, I pulled out my phone and opened up the attachment I'd previously left closed. The details of the single residential purple fire Rick had found. My vision blurred as my eyes read the address.

"Marissa, tell me what's going on."

I handed over my phone for him to look at, though I knew the numbers wouldn't mean anything to him. Not like they did to me. In a dull monotone, I explained, "These addresses do have something in common. Me." Before they could bombard me with questions, I explained. "The foster care office that burned down? I was in their system. This address..." I pointed to Koda's phone and the image of the scribbles. "The house that burned down thirty years ago, it's the same one from the file I found about myself. It's where I was found."

"A fire set by the chimera," Koda murmured.

"How did you survive?" Ambrose's tone lilted in curiosity.

I shrugged. "No idea. The authorities found me in the ashes, naked and unharmed. Despite them questioning me, all I knew was my name. Marissa. And my age. Five. Which I'm thinking I might have gotten wrong, based on the hospital burning six years previous. In any case, I didn't know how I'd gotten there, or even who my parents were."

"At that age, it's possible you didn't know your last name, or your parents' names," Koda mused aloud. "It's also not uncommon for children to only refer to their parent as mom or dad."

"I also couldn't tell them how I came to be there or what happened. It's like my memories were wiped."

"No one ever came forth to claim you?" Orion's brows rose high on his forehead.

I shook my head. "Nope and no database DNA ever matched mine."

"And this other address?" Koda inquired, pointing to my phone with Rick's report.

"Used to be my foster home. I got sent there after Cryptid Youth Services satisfied themselves that I wouldn't cause harm."

"Don't tell me they thought you might have set the fire you were found in?" Orion jumped in.

"They didn't know what to think. Here I was, in the still-smoldering ashes, with no real memory or explanation nor a single burn. They ran extensive tests on me, only to realize I was an ordinary human and not a cryptid."

"Hardly ordinary given you're a witch," Koda pointed out.

I could only offer a faint smile. "A witch with an unidentified bloodline and muddied past. Luckily, Hekate didn't care."

"That is our goddess," Ambrose stated with pride. "She isn't one to discriminate. Magic is magic."

Koda squeezed my leg. "Sounds like a tough childhood."

"Not as tough as some. I lucked out in that my foster family actually cared for the kids they took in. Not everyone is that lucky." I'd been donating clothes and other gear to the Cryptid Foster Care Society ever since I started working full-time. I was grateful for a system that took care of me and hoped to give back.

Ambrose stood and paced. "Is it me, or do some of

these fires seem like their purpose was to erase Marissa's existence?"

I blinked at him. "Why would you say that?"

"Because they obscured your roots, and in turn, no one ever figured out your identity." Orion pointed out.

"Why would anyone do that?" Koda asked.

"You should know solving a case involves finding the coincidences."

"I think you're reaching," he scoffed.

"Am I?" I countered. "There's the CA science lab fire. It supposedly had a magical glitch that torched their records, but want to bet that's where I was tested?"

He frowned. "I guess it's possible. But wouldn't those records have been backed up on a computer network?"

"In a perfect world, yes. But guess what? Right before we were assigned this case I was working on entering thirty years' worth of precinct files that someone decided to throw in a storage unit instead of digitizing. Turns out, the CA and file maintenance? Not so great."

"I think you're grasping." He picked my phone back up and I watched him flip through the attachments of Rick's reports. "Do you know the car dealership that got hit by the arsonist? Or the clothing store right after? Have you visited a motel by the name of Quickie Dickie?"

"I'm not saying they're all connected to me—the mobile phone store sure isn't—but maybe the fire starter burned down other places to try to throw us off. In any case, those places all happen to be on a direct route from the prison the chimera escaped from to here."

It was Ambrose who made me stiffen by asking, "Are you by any chance related to the chimera?"

"No. Don't be silly. I'm a witch." The very idea sounded preposterous.

"But you said it yourself. You were an orphan with no roots, so it's possible," Orion countered.

"I can't shift into a chimera shape. Nor is my magical fire blue."

"Could be you take after your father," Ambrose suggested.

"No. The chimera is not my mother." Me, descended from a dangerous cryptid who was responsible for the house fire where I was found? Never. My blood work had me as human in origin.

"A good agent doesn't discount possibilities so quickly," Koda stated. "We have two known blue fires. One being the house where you were found and the other a hospital records room. Based on the conclusions you've already drawn, I think we can safely bet they had a log of your birth."

My lips pressed tight. "I think I'd know if a criminal was my parent. And before you tell me I'm being emotional, the fact is all cryptids who are incarcerated have their DNA scanned. Given how often they checked to see if I had relatives, it would have pinged." Yet even as I said it, the image of the chimera's heavily redacted file sprung to mind. All those black boxes covering all those hidden truths...

"Unless the fires aren't the only way someone was actively hiding your existence," Koda interjected.

"Why?" I exclaimed.

"Could it be because they knew the chimera would come looking and wanted to keep you safe?" Ambrose offered a reason, but I remained unconvinced.

"Let's say you're right about me being related to the chimera, which I don't think you are, by the way. Why would someone go through the trouble of hiding me, only to turn around and try to kill me at Lenora's house?" I attacked the flaw in his logic.

"Because we're not dealing with one person," Koda mused aloud. "At the start of the case, we assumed we had the chimera starting the fires, the person who put out the bounty for the chimera, and someone hiding the chimera."

"And now, what? Are you saying that whoever hid the chimera also hid me?"

"I'm saying there could be someone who was hiding the chimera's info and someone else hiding your info, or it could be one person who wasn't protecting the chimera by redacting her file, but protecting you by making sure no one could prove a connection between you two."

"Because the chimera tried to murder me in that house fire and no one wanted her to know she didn't finish the job." There was no proof of it, yet it seemed to be where the evidence pointed. "Now she's somehow learned that I survived, and she's coming for me."

"Not necessarily." Koda spoke in a no-nonsense detective voice, even though we talked about me being specifically targeted for murder.

"Oh, okay, What else could it be?" I tried to keep my nerves in check but failed. "Let's not forget we also have the person who put out the bounty. They want the chimera captured, probably so they can torture her for revenge. Could be that they might have made the same stupid guess that I'm related to the chimera and thought, why not go after me, too."

"At least in that scenario the chimera probably cares about you and isn't a cold-blooded daughter murderer."

I couldn't help but grimace. "I really wish you'd stop implying I'm her daughter. I'd rather not be related to a monster."

"We still don't know what she actually did," Koda reminded.

"We know I was found in the remains of a house that burned down in blue flames. We know chimera's flames burn blue. We know the chimera was in a supermax prison, had her existence wiped, even her file redacted. Whatever she did must have been bad."

Orion piped in. "Better hope she's got a maternal instinct then, because if your boyfriend is right, one way or another she's coming for you."

"It does seem like that," Koda agreed.

"How do you figure?" Denial seemed to be my only

"On second thought, Ambrose is right. I shouldn't be putting you in danger," Koda's tight reply.

"Not up to you, and don't forget, this is our job. We capture cryptids. It's what we've trained to do. And at least, now, we kind of know what to expect. Since the arsonist relies on fire, I'll work on ways to extinguish and render them impotent. I can check the spell-casting database for some techniques."

"Don't be so quick to assume we can handle it. We have no idea what the chimera is capable of," Koda reminded.

"Then it's a good thing you'll be around to protect me. You and the Hounds."

My solution only made Koda's grimace deeper, but Hekate's pets?

Ambrose grinned widely, and Orion fist-pumped. "Bring on the hunt. *Awoo!*"

CHAPTER 13

Koda didn't usually have an issue setting up traps. He excelled at them after all; he usually could outsmart those he hunted. The use of bait? Again, part of his strategy, however, it became wholly different when the woman he found himself falling for wanted to put herself out there to draw danger.

Right away, Marissa was ready to dive in and dangle herself in the open.

She held a can of cola in one hand as she paced, talking aloud. "So the person who set fire to Lenora's place thinks I'm dead. Even if they don't, they must be wondering where I am. Since you cloaked my movements, they don't know I'm here. At the same time, we don't want to draw them to my boss's house. We'll have to relocate. Maybe the hotel where you've been staying." She tossed the latter part of that at Koda. "It's walking distance to the precinct, so plenty of opportunity for them to make a move."

friend at this point. The only way I was going to save myself from becoming the target—or maybe even worse, the daughter—of a monster. "I'm like what, a two-, three-day drive from where she escaped? It's been almost a year since the prisoners escaped. More than enough time for her to get here if that's what she wanted."

"You're talking about someone with no money, who's been in jail for three decades. Could be she wasn't sure where to find you. Maybe she can't drive." Koda gave reasons, and I shot them down.

"There's buses."

"Where she might be seen and reported. And don't forget, she's a fugitive with a bounty on her head. She knows she has an enemy, that someone is actively hunting her, so she has to be careful. Maybe she waited until she thought things had calmed down and she could roll into town unnoticed." Koda kept insisting.

I sighed. "This is crazy."

"It is, but this is also the break we've been waiting for. Right now, whoever attacked you at Lenora's house thinks you're dead. You need to make a public appearance, alive and well, before the chimera leaves town."

"Is your boyfriend suggesting we use you as bait? That's cold, man," Ambrose exclaimed.

I jumped to his defense. "No, because he's right. I only have two choices, hide or set a trap. I know what I prefer."

"Too many ways that could go wrong," Koda grumbled. "You're well aware we can't act overtly or the humans will panic." While humanity knew of cryptids and those with magic, they didn't like it when it affected their daily life or things got a little too weird—or violent.

Unperturbed by his caution, she waved a hand. "Thus far, the attacks have been discreet. No reason to think that will change."

"Burning buildings down hasn't exactly been discreet," he reminded.

"None of them resulted in casualties. They were done after business hours, or when the houses were empty."

"Not including you and Lenora."

"You know what I mean."

"Don't forget we're dealing with an unknown amount of people, though."

"If you're right," she challenged. "I'm not convinced. It could be the person hiding chimera's existence is behind the bounty as well."

"Either way, we have to be careful and not too cocky. Being good at our jobs means not taking unnecessary risks and being prepared."

Her lips quirked. "Or flinging magic at it and seeing what sticks."

"A good peeing sometimes works," Orion chimed in, earning yet another glare.

Koda could have done without the pair of hounds, but they gave Marissa extra protection that he could count on, so he begrudgingly accepted them onto the team.

"You know," Ambrose said, finally adding to the conversation, "Instead of waiting for Marissa to be attacked, why not go after the person offering the bounty?"

"We've already talked about that. Doubtful anyone offering a bounty on the dark web is going to want to talk to law enforcement," Koda pointed out.

"But what if we pretended to have caught her?" Ambrose explained. "We make contact claiming we've captured the chimera."

"They'll want proof," Koda argued.

Ambrose glanced at Marissa. "You saw a partial of the chimera, correct?" At her nod, he added, "Could you create an illusion that we could use to convince the bounty poster?"

"Yes, but in order for it to work, I'd have to cast it on someone, and I should warn, I don't know how well it would withstand scrutiny up close."

"We don't need it to be seamless, just good enough to provide video proof to the bounty poster," Ambrose explained.

Koda actually warmed to the idea. "We provide a passable decoy and get the bounty poster to reveal themselves, which either eliminates the threat entirely or, at the least, removes an active player."

"When should we contact them?" was Marissa's next question.

No time like the present. It didn't take long for her to recreate the image she'd seen of the chimera. Given they'd not seen her full face, they made the illusion with the same kind of hooded trench coat seen in the memory rewind they'd viewed.

Since they couldn't be sure if the person offering the bounty knew about Koda, they used Ambrose in the video proof they sent on the dark web. He held the end of a leash that hooked to a collar around Marissa's neck. Wearing her magical illusion, she had her hands tucked in front of her, in matching shackles. Her head bowed for most of the recording, until the very end, when she lifted it and showed off the one brilliant blue eye and a peek of matching hair.

"Awesome. This looks perfect." Orion proved to be full of enthusiasm.

Koda actually agreed and soon had the video and the message firing off to the person offering the bounty. The reply came quickly, which kind of sucked. Koda had been hoping to get Marissa alone. He fooled himself into thinking it would be to talk. In reality? He wanted to devour those lips and hear her panting as she undulated under him again.

As if catching his thoughts, she turned at that moment and smiled at him. A soft and sensual promise on her lips and in her eyes.

He went instantly hard and wanted to curse that the meeting would take place within the hour. It seemed too fast.

Abe returned to his house as the team prepared to leave for the designated meeting spot. He took one look at the disguised Marissa and recoiled, leaving Koda to quickly shout, "It's not the chimera!"

Abe remained stiff as he asked, "Then who is it?"

"It's me, boss." Marissa waved. "This is just a disguise. We're about to go meet the person offering the bounty."

Kowalski scowled. "You were just gassed and left for dead in a house fire. You shouldn't be running off doing stunts like this."

"I don't need to tell you that I'm not the sort of agent to sit on the sidelines when things start getting good."

"Given the attacks, we needed to do something. This will get one player out of the way," Koda explained.

Abe's expression pinched. "Can it wait? I need Agent Smith for something."

"We can't reschedule the meeting, or they'll know something is up. Can I help you after?" Marissa offered as a compromise.

"You might not want to wait once you hear the reason why." Abe paused and said, "We got a hit on your biological mother in the cryptid database."

Marissa swayed, and as Koda grabbed her, the illusion she wore melted away.

"You found her?" was her faint reply.

Abe nodded. "I've got her coming in for questioning. She doesn't know why. I thought you'd want to be there."

"I do, but I'm supposed to help in the sting operation." Marissa's stricken expression tore at Koda.

"What if you turned me into the chimera?" Koda offered her a solution. "I'll go in your place."

"But—" She bit her lower lip, and Orion jumped in. "Don't worry. Me and Ambrose will keep your boyfriend safe. The three of us can handle whatever is coming."

"Don't be so sure. Lenora called the attacker evil, and we know they have magic and aren't afraid to use it," she reminded.

"That's assuming the bounty poster is the arsonist. Could be they're benign," Koda pointed out.

"Is this a good time to mention Hekate's blessing allows us to absorb most spells?" Orion grinned. "You ain't seen anything funnier than the look on a warlock's face when he throws a massive fireball thinking he'd going to evaporate you, only to find himself getting nipped in the ball sac."

"Are you sure?" The dog's quips fell on deaf ears as Koda focused on Marissa, watching her sense of duty war with that of hope.

Koda couldn't take that from her. Not when he'd witnessed how distraught she'd been at the idea that her mother could be a monster. "Go. Find the answers to your past. We'll meet you there in a few hours once we've taken the bounty poster into custody."

"Thank you!" Her bright smile made him wish he could go with her, stay at her side and offer support. Alas, he needed to go because if the hounds absorbed spells, then that left only him capable of wearing the disguise.

Koda checked the clock on the wall. "We'll leave in ten minutes. So do whatever you need to, but be ready."

"I was born ready," Orion boasted.

"He means take a piss," Ambrose growled.

"I don't have to piss."

"So if I say picture a waterfall..."

"I fucking hate you," Orion snarled as he stalked out of the house. A smirking Ambrose followed.

Abe frowned. "Why are they going outside?"

"I'm thinking to water your bushes," Koda remarked with a straight face.

The statement deepened Abe's scowl. "Fucking canines, always marking shit. I'm going to get the hose." Abe stalked off, leaving Koda alone with Marissa.

"Are you going to be okay?" He grabbed her hands and squeezed.

"I could ask the same of you. I don't like letting you go off into danger alone."

"Hardly alone. I've got Frick and Frack with me."

Her lips curved. "They're not that bad."

"You haven't spent as much time with them. They are like a pair of squabbling children."

"Hekate wouldn't have sent them if they were useless."

He sighed. "I'm sure they'll be useful, just annoying."

"I'll have to make it up to you later," she purred, tucking herself close to his chest.

"I like the sound of that." He lifted her so their lips could be level. But before he kissed her, he said, "Be careful."

"Ditto." She ran her fingertips down his cheek. "I'll need you in working condition for what I have planned."

"What do you have planned?"

"Something naked, orgasmic, and fun." She winked.

He hardened and couldn't help but kiss her.

A kiss that had them both panting and might have not ended but for Orion's bellowed, "Ten minutes are going by fast, lover boy. Let's get this show on the road."

He gave her a rueful smile. "Later?"

"Definitely," her vehement reply. "Now stand still while I make you into the chimera."

Her magic tingled as it settled over him. "This glamour won't withstand touch," she explained. "It can be shattered if you're not careful."

Which meant he'd be screwed. A skinwalker could only replicate animals. Not humans. An odd quirk of his kind, unlike doppelgangers, which only mimicked humanity.

He left with the hounds, wearing a collar and a leash, his hands wrapped in shackles that appeared sturdy but could be easily yanked apart. He resisted the urge to turn around and look. No need. He felt her watching as he drove away, and a part of him screamed to go back.

She's in danger.

A danger he'd hopefully end within the hour.

CHAPTER 14

Koda left to confront the bounty poster, and a part of me wished I'd gone with him, not because he truly needed my help but because I found myself wanting to be by his side. My lips still tingled—as did other parts—and I found myself excited to see what would happen next with him. Did we have a future? I kind of wanted to explore that, but first, I had to deal with the fluttery fear and excitement at finally getting to meet my mother.

Would she have a good reason for having abandoned me? Would I hate her on sight? Burst into tears? It should be noted, I rarely cried. I tried to not let things get me down, but at the same time, part of that forced determination to be if not happy but content came from my messed-up childhood. Would the answers I might get today help or worsen my mental state? Guess I'd soon find out.

My inner musings got shelved as Kowalski entered the room looking tense.

"You okay, boss?"

"Yeah, but I'm rethinking my invitation to Hekate's pets. I thought they'd be housebroken," he complained. "My roses are delicate."

"I'll have a chat with them."

He waved a hand. "Don't worry about that. We have more important things to attend."

"You really think you found my bio mom?" I asked.

"The DNA doesn't lie," Kowalski chirped.

"It's not the chimera, is it?" I cringed as I voiced the fear aloud.

"What makes you say that?"

"Just some oddities I've come across from my childhood. The guys seem to think there's a possibility." I shook my head. "But that's just crazy. I mean the chimera has been in the system for decades. Someone would have made the connection before now."

"Then I guess you've got your answer."

"How did you happen to come across my mother? How did she get added to the cryptid DNA database? Is she a criminal?" It would be ironic considering I'd gotten a career in law enforcement.

"Why don't we get going first, and I can explain on the way."

I glanced at my outfit, crumpled and somewhat grimy. "I don't suppose you have anything in my size to borrow?"

"I doubt she'll care about your appearance."

"Assuming she cares about me at all," I countered as I followed him outside. He didn't bother locking the door, most likely to allow Koda and the dogs entry when they returned. "Maybe she doesn't even remember me."

"Oh, she remembers," his low drawl as he got into the driver's seat.

I popped in beside him and clipped by belt before questioning, "So she's aware she has a daughter?"

"Yes."

"Did she say why she left me?" I asked as he put the car into gear and reversed from his driveway.

"She had no choice because she went to jail."

Ouch. It stung to find out my bio mom was a criminal. Ouch. "What did she do?"

"A bunch of things. Grand larceny, murder, arson."

I flinched with each charge and started to wonder if I really wanted to meet this woman. Maybe it would be better not knowing her. "Guess her being arrested explains why she never came back for me. But prisoners still have rights. Didn't she ask to see me?"

"She never told anyone of your existence."

One thing did perturb. "I'm kind of surprised it took this long to make the connection. I mean, she would have been arrested thirty-some years ago, meaning when they ran my DNA they should have gotten a match."

"Mistakes happen. Turns out the DNA we had on file for her belonged to someone else."

"Seriously?" A technical error was to blame for me living my whole life in the dark?

"These things happen more often than you'd think. Vials get mixed up or contaminated."

"I wasn't aware you knew about my past," I stated. It wasn't something I hid, but I didn't go out of my way to tell people either.

"I made it a point to research all the staff before coming on board."

Kowalski took the on-ramp for the highway, and I clued in we weren't heading for the precinct. "Where are we going? I thought we were meeting my mom at the office."

"Not quite. I had a feeling you wouldn't want your first moment with her to be a spectacle for everyone to spy on, so I arranged a different spot that would provide more privacy. One that you might even remember from your time with your mom."

"Don't be so sure. I lost all my memories of that time." Except in my dreams, which I couldn't remember but for the flames. When I woke, for a second, I'd feel as if I knew, and then it would slip away.

"Guess we'll soon find out."

Because of his cryptic replies, I half-expected our final destination. There was only one place that Kowalski would have known about that might have once housed me and my mother.

The house that burned down. The one where I'd been orphaned.

I'd never once visited it, not even as an adult, since I'd never known the address—not until I'd found my file. I wondered if things had been different, if the file hadn't been lost, would I have been able to visit and trigger memories? A part of me recoiled from that idea. Considered it the place where I lost my life. Where I had to become someone new. Little orphan Marissa.

I didn't realize my hands shook until I emerged from the car and surveilled the ruined lot. No one had rebuilt on the site, the concrete foundation all that remained, cracked in spots with weeds sprouting. The houses on the street all appeared condemned, boarded over and forlorn.

The housing shortage and lack of rentals made me wonder how this area could have been allowed to fall into such disrepair. "What happened?"

"After the fire, people just started moving out, and none ever returned. Some claimed the place had a curse."

A shiver went through me, and I hugged myself. I understood their dislike of the area. I wanted nothing more than to run away. It took effort to not get back in that car and demand we leave.

"When is she supposed to meet us?"

"Soon. I wanted to get here early and set the stage for the reunion. After all, it's been decades. You're a grown woman now."

As I moved up the overgrown walkway, the concrete slabs cracked in spots, I found myself asking, "When was she released from prison?"

"She wasn't. She escaped."

At the admission, I whirled. "Wait, is this a trap to arrest her and send her back?"

"I'm not planning to arrest her. I have other plans."

My newest shiver had little to do with the location and everything to do with the sly smile on Kowalski's face.

A creepy-as-fuck smile.

And suddenly, a memory unlocked. Just as I had at Lorena's, but this time without the dogs amplifying my magic, I pulled out the memories of this place, combining it with my own past that had been locked up and hidden inside my own mind.

And I plunged us into a nightmare.

The popcorn smelled so good. I watched Mommy as she pulled it from the microwave, the bag inflated with crunchy, salty goodness.

I clapped my hands. "Yay."

Mommy tossed me a bright smile. "It won't be long, baby. Let me get a bowl and then we can snuggle and watch a movie."

Mommy rented Jumanji, *and I couldn't wait to see it. I loved our snuggle time.*

"Why don't you grab us each a can of cola?" A treat reserved for our movie nights.

"Okay." I went to the fridge and heaved hard to open it.

I heard a clatter and turned around to see the bowl upside down on the floor and popcorn strewn everywhere.

"Oh no," I exclaimed.

Mommy looked horrified as well. "Baby, you need to hide."

"Why?"

"The bad man is here."

Instantly, I froze. Mommy had told me stories about the bad man. How he would hurt us if he ever found us. Every house we lived in, Mommy taught me where to go and hide. We even practiced with Mommy hugging me after and whispering, "I'll never let anyone hurt you."

Why would someone hurt me? I'd asked my mommy, and she always looked sad when she said, "Some people are just plain evil."

"Quickly," Mommy exhorted. "He can't find you."

"But—" Tears welled and threatened to spill.

Mommy grabbed me in a tight hug, squeezing me close before whispering, "I won't let him hurt you. Now go."

I sniffled and sobbed as I went to the cubby she'd built for me under the stairs. I had my hand on the latch when I heard a voice booming.

"I know you're in there. Come outside, Calliope."

"Why can't you leave me alone?" Mommy sounded angry.

"You know I can't do that. We were meant to be."

"You're deluded," she exclaimed. Despite her warning, I crept to the window and peeked out. A man stood there, tall but skinny. He had long hair tied back in a ponytail and a mean face. A scary face.

"I don't know why you insist on making this so difficult. Or is it that you love the chase?"

"Fuck off," Mommy snapped, and my eyes widened. Mommy never cussed.

"Such language," he huffed. "I'm thinking some time in solitary might be just what you need to adjust your attitude."

"Go to Hell," Mommy stated and flung out her hands. To my shock, blue fire emerged from her fingertips, but it didn't hit the man. An invisible shield stopped it.

The man offered her a nasty smile. "My turn."

I didn't see what he did, but it made my mommy scream. I almost ran out. I had my hand on the doorknob when I heard her in my head.

Hide, baby. Hide before he hurts you too.

I ran for my cubby, this time getting inside and shutting it tight, placing my hands over my ears to avoid hearing my mommy's cries of pain. Tears rolled down my cheeks. Fear made me pee my pants.

Mommy's voice spoke again inside my head. Don't be afraid. The flames are your friend. The flames will help you forget. The flames will hide you.

I didn't understand what she meant until the cubby got hot and smoke seeped inside.

Fire!

In my panic, I tried to get out of the cubby, but I couldn't get the latch to work. Couldn't get the door to open.

Sleep, baby. Sleep and forget.

At her command, I closed my eyes, and when next I opened them, I was alone.

I snapped out of the memory and gaped at Kowalski.

"You were the bad man my mom was trying to hide me from."

"And she did a good job too. Her last act before I captured her was not just to burn down the house with evidence of your existence but to enchant the smoke from it with a spell of forgetfulness. I never knew you existed until I saw your agent profile picture. You're the spitting image of her, you know, minus the hair and eyes. It was then I knew. Knew she'd come for you when she escaped."

"You're using me as bait." My stomach clenched.

"Surprise!" Kowalski smirked. "She surrendered to me once before to save your life. Wanna bet she'll do it again?"

She would. I finally remembered. Remembered the love she had for me. The sacrifice she made to protect.

Now it was my turn to protect her. I just wished I knew how. My hand shoved into my pocket as if it would suddenly have a gun, but all my fingers found were a sugar packet.

But did Koda have the matching ketchup one?

CHAPTER 15

Koda shifted on the park bench, uneasy, and yet he couldn't have said why.

Not entirely true. He worried about Marissa. He second-guessed his choice to come to this park rather than accompanying her while she met the mother who'd abandoned her.

Something about the situation nagged. How had Abe found Marissa's mother? Why had he even been looking? Abe had only known Marissa for a few months, and Koda doubted she would have spoken about her childhood to her boss.

"Someone's coming," Ambrose hissed, pulling him from his thoughts.

Indeed, a form, in a long billowing cloak, strode across the baseball diamond, head covered in a hood. He walked like a fighter, the swagger confident. As he neared, features became visible within the cowl. A square jaw, a nose at a slight angle as if it had been broken a few times, a scar that ran from the lip across the cheek to the temple.

Still in his magical disguise, Koda rose from the bench, the hood of his sweater hiding most of his features. Ambrose stood with him, holding the fake leash.

The stranger paused a few paces away and waited in silence.

Ambrose broke the impasse. "I've brought the chimera. Where's the money?"

The stranger crossed his arms. "There is no reward because this is not she."

Koda stiffened.

Unperturbed, Ambrose snorted. "Is this how you do business? Because that's bullshit. Cost me quite a bit to collar this one, and I expect compensation. If not from you, then someone will pay."

"I see the greed of humanity hasn't changed."

"Who says I'm human?" taunted Ambrose.

The man cocked his head, and his lips curved slightly. "My mistake. Who do you serve?"

"The goddess Hekate, and she won't be happy if you mess with her favorite hound," Ambrose declared.

"I have no argument with the goddess, but I do take issue with lies." The man waved a hand, and Koda didn't have to look down at himself to know the glamour had dropped. "Is Hekate now working with my enemy?"

Since Koda no longer had to pretend, he felt free to ask, "What enemy?"

"The one who sent me away to die," the man growled.

"Who are you?" Koda asked because he suddenly found himself curious. This was not unfolding as expected. While the man cut an imposing figure, Koda got no sense of menace.

"I am Kratos. And you?"

"Koda. And this is my companion, Ambrose."

"And the other one hiding over by the play structure?" Kratos waved a hand.

"That's Orion, another of Hekate's hounds," Koda explained, realizing that, whoever they faced, he wasn't human.

Orion stepped out, huffing, "How did you see me? I had my scent hidden."

"I didn't survive decades in Tartarus to be fooled by such childish tricks," Kratos offered with a smirk.

Tartarus? "Hold on, that place is real?" Koda had heard of it. A place where misbehaving gods supposedly got sent, guarded by fearsome titans and monsters.

"Real enough to scar me and keep me trapped for much too long." Kratos grimaced. "Now, enough of your questions. Time to answer mine. Where is Calliope?"

"Who?"

"The chimera."

At last, a name. "I don't know," Koda admitted. "We set this trap to capture you so you'd stop trying to kill Marissa."

"Who is Marissa?" Kratos sounded genuinely confused.

"Why do you want the chimera?" Koda countered.

"That is none of your business."

"I'd say it is, considering the efforts being made to conceal her whereabouts and the attacks on those of us trying to find her."

"I've attacked no one, and why would I hide her location when I want to find her?" Kratos didn't hide his exasperation.

"Find her why?"

"That is between me and her," snapped the man.

"Have you been setting fires?" Orion point-blank asked.

"No. That's not one of my skills. I am a warrior. I live by the sword." A sword he suddenly showed off by pulling from a sheath down his back.

"Damn, dude, that's a big knife," Orion whistled.

"And it will carve you up if I don't get answers," growled Kratos.

"Trust me, we'd like some too. I'm beginning to think we need to get some things straight." Because things didn't add up. "I've been tasked by the Cryptid Authority, along with my partner, Marissa, to find the chimera who escaped from prison."

"Prison?" The man sounded surprised. "For what crime?"

"No one seems to know."

"You said Calliope escaped. Where is she now?" Kratos asked.

"We think she's in the area because of a possible connection to Marissa."

"You keep saying that name. Who is this Marissa, and why would you think Calliope has an interest?"

"That's what we're trying to figure out. Marissa's an orphan, found at a young age in the remains of a fire set by the chimera."

Kratos shook his head. "Calliope would never harm a child."

"Never said she was hurt. Marissa emerged unscathed but with no memories of her past. Although she might get those answers soon. Abe is taking her to meet her mother."

"I care not about these people. I want to find Calliope. The advertisement I placed was supposed to help, not waste my time on strangers." Kratos turned to leave, and Koda barked, "Not so fast. I'm not done asking questions."

"As if I care. I'm only interested in finding Calliope."

"Why? Why are you so interested in her? Are you planning to kill her?"

"Never!" The vehemence vibrated in the air. "I love her."

It was Ambrose who began putting the pieces together. "Someone tossed you in Tartarus because of your relationship with her."

Kratos' expression darkened. "Prometheus couldn't accept she chose me. I would have killed him, but even demi-gods aren't easy to kill, and so we did our best to evade detection. Lived happily for many years until Prometheus found us. We fought, but he cheated. He cast a dark spell that flung me into Tartarus, where he assumed I'd die. He forgot he wasn't the only one with some god blood." Kratos' chin lifted. "Every day in that place I had to fight to stay alive. Spent decades searching for an escape. Now that I've returned, I've been trying to find Calliope, but that bastard has obscured her location."

"Okay, cool story. Back to Marissa, though? Is she your kid?" Trust Orion to be blunt.

Without hesitation, Kratos stated, "We had no children."

"Are you sure about that?" Ambrose queried. "Because the evidence we have seems to indicate the chimera tried to hide the fact she had a baby, and that said baby is Marissa."

The man pursed his lips. "It is possible she carried my child but didn't know before I was imprisoned. Take me to her and I will know the truth."

On a whim, Koda said, "Can you take off your hood?"

"Why?"

"To see the color of your hair."

The man grimaced. "Why does it matter?" he complained and yet pushed back the cowl.

Koda stared, and Ambrose huffed, "It's the same shade as Marissa's."

The remark widened Kratos' eyes. "The child has pink hair?"

"Hardly a child. She's thirty-five."

"And I've been gone for almost thirty-six years," the shell-shocked man murmured.

"This person you say has been stalking the chimera, does he happen to like fire?" Koda questioned.

"Yes. Prometheus has always liked to burn things. The first time he kidnapped Calliope, he torched everything she touched so I couldn't track her. Luckily, my love managed to escape."

Ambrose turned to Koda. "I'm thinking Prometheus must be the other player who's been setting all those fires."

"You think he knows Marissa is the chimera's kid?" Koda mused aloud.

"It would explain the attacks." Ambrose turned to Kratos. "I don't suppose you know where this Prometheus is?"

"If I did, he'd be dead." A flat and dark reply.

"A better question is, what does this Prometheus look like? Do you have a picture?" Orion interjected.

A frown creased Kratos' brow. "No. But I well recall his appearance. Let me see if my meager magic can conjure it for you to see." The man held out his hand and concentrated, his brow furrowing even deeper. "I'm too weak on this plane."

"Hold on, I might be able to help." Orion held out his hand, and Kratos eyed it as if it were slimy. "Grab it and I can boost your magic, courtesy of my goddess."

The man appeared ready to refuse, but with a

grunt, he clasped it. The moment he did, the air before him shimmered. It coalesced into a shape. A man with long hair tied back and a sneer.

A man Koda knew.

"Fuck me! That's Abe."

"Wait, isn't that the guy whose house we're staying at?" Orion asked with surprise.

"Yes. And he took Marissa to meet her mom." Koda's stomach clenched.

Ambrose took over this train of thought to murmur, "And if her mom is the chimera, then he's using her as bait."

"Or a hostage." Koda kicked the ground and cursed. "How the fuck did he manage to fool us?"

"The more important thing is, where did he take her?" Ambrose pointed out.

"What the fuck?" Koda got distracted as the pocket in his pants began to ooze. A shove of his hand inside pulled out an exploded ketchup packet, the one Marissa hexed. As he touched it, Koda suddenly knew where to find her. "Abe's taken her to the house that burned down when she was a child."

"We must make haste," Kratos declared, sheathing his sword. "Take me at once."

"To the hound mobile!" Orion chirped as he headed for the car, which would be subject to lights and traffic.

Koda had a better idea. "You drive. I'll meet you there."

"How? You can't exactly run faster," Ambrose reminded.

"No, but I can fly." And his internal navigation would direct the way.

The question being, would he get there in time?

CHAPTER 16

Facing off against the man who'd ruined my life left me with a big question. "Why do you hate my mother so much?"

"Hate? On the contrary. I would have showered her with anything she wanted. Given her the world if she demanded. But she wanted another." Kowalski's lips turned down.

Not the answer I'd expected. "You were in love with my mother?"

"Still am. Which is why you're still alive. What better gift than to give Calliope the daughter she thought lost? You know, when I discovered your existence, my first impulse was to kill you. After all, you were a reminder of her betrayal. But then it occurred to me, what better way to lure your mother than by dangling her daughter?"

"You're assuming a lot. I haven't seen her in decades. I doubt she'd give up her freedom for me."

"Says how little you know of a mother's love. Everything she did was to protect you. She destroyed the record of your birth. That fire you were found in? A way of erasing your existence. How lucky for you I was long gone when you were found, or you might not be standing here today, about to hand me the thing I most desire."

"I find it hard to believe you love her," I retorted. "You put her in prison."

"She left me no choice. She refused to listen to reason. It was my hope that she would realize after some time alone that I was the better choice."

"But she never did," I murmured. "She spent thirty years in jail rather than give in to your sick desire."

"I'm not sick," he hissed. "She was supposed to be mine. We were happy until *he* came along. *He* stole her from me. Tainted her with his touch and seed."

In other words, my mom dared to love another. "What happened to my father?"

Kowalski's grin turned malicious as he chortled, "Sent him to a place even gods fear. I doubt he lived more than a day or two. With him gone, your mother should have been mine."

"I can see why she ran. You can't force someone to love you."

"That's what you think."

"How do you know she's coming here? I highly doubt she called you up to set up a meeting."

"Actually, she did." He smirked. "That cell phone she stole? She wanted it so she could contact me and tell me how she would enjoy killing me slowly. It only took telling her that I was now her precious daughter's boss for her to finally deign to speak to me."

"How *did* you come to be my boss?"

"I'd worked for the CA for years, how do you think I was able to put your mom in that prison with such a redacted history? Anyway, the recent corruption scandal put your town on the map. Everyone in the CA was talking about it. Word spread, and I couldn't believe it when I saw your profile photo included on that list of agents who'd made it through the cut—as I've already said, you look just like her. A little bit of research told me that you were an orphan, so there was no doubt in my mind about who your mother really was and why Calliope had stayed in the area. I immediately put my name in to take over your precinct."

"She was looking for me," I concluded. "But I don't understand something. Who was covering up my connection to the chimera after she went to prison? Why didn't my DNA match to hers?"

"Dumb luck." He scoffed. "I mean, lucky for you. Had I known of your existence I absolutely would have claimed you. That would have forced Calliope to accept my proposal. Alas, chimera have two sets of DNA—did you know that? I didn't, back then. Thirty years ago we weren't very knowledgeable about DNA. If we were, I would have ensured both sets were on record. My only misstep, really."

"Not sure I'd agree with that being your *only*

misstep," I muttered. "Why all the fires? Were you trying to get the CA to think they were caused by her so you could arrest her?"

"Not even close. Fires are how I've always expressed myself to her, ever since she first tried to leave. They're my calling card, my love letter. It's how I tell her that I still want her. And that no matter where she goes, I'm watching. Waiting for her to give herself to me."

"You're a sick fuck." I felt like vomiting. "If you're so cocky and confident that she'll give herself to you, then why put up a bounty? Just to cover your bases?"

"Of course not." His face twisted at that. "That one wasn't me. I can only assume that's some hot-headed CA agent trying to make a name for themselves by capturing fugitives, which is why I stayed on top of removing any mentions of a chimera from the World Wide Web. I can't imagine who else would be offering bounties like that."

I couldn't either.

For some reason, I suddenly thought of the page Lenora translated. The woman with the stalker, who had to keep moving because she couldn't escape a madman. That woman was my mother. And the stalker was *him*. That's why the page appeared in the library after my spell. I'd just not grasped the connection to the case until now.

"You knew about the diary."

"What diary?" he looked genuinely confused.

Perhaps Lenora was right, and the gargoyles had found it and brought it there all on their own.

"You didn't know about the diary? Then why destroy the hidden gargoyle library?"

"I assumed she was watching you." He shrugged. "And burning down places is how I showed her my love."

"You bastard." Not just for stalking my mother, but also for destroying so much knowledge, and those poor endangered gargoyles. "What about the clerk? Why kill him?"

"Just in case." He wrinkled his nose. "Damn he was chatty, and he had no problem letting you sift around in his perverted little brain. What if you decided that you wanted to see more from that night? I couldn't risk you reviewing the memories and catching me in his shop around the same time your mother was inside the phone store."

My mouth dropped open. We hadn't thought to ask the clerk to show us the rest of the store. Though, Abe didn't have the equipment that interested the guy, so he probably hadn't made an imprint in the memory. The poor clerk really had died for nothing.

But that final confession only strengthened my determination. "I won't let you have her." Gathering my magic, I threw a massive ball of electricity that crackled and fizzled. It should have if not killed him, at least zapped him into unconsciousness.

Kowalski caught it. Cradled my sphere of destruction in the palm of his hand and grinned. "You'll have to do better than that." He then popped it into his mouth and chewed.

I blinked. That shouldn't have been possible. It led to me blurting out, "What are you?"

"A god. A minor one, according to history books, who are so obsessed with the bigger ones like Zeus and Hera." He rolled his eyes. "Which is fine. I like people underestimating me."

I took a step back as I realized the trouble I was in. Gods were almost impossible to kill. A witch might be powerful, but we remained no match for a deity. I needed to get away from him.

My next blast of magic acted more as a diversion than an actual attack. I used the sudden explosion of obscuring fog to run. I made it only a few paces before a fist of force grabbed me.

I couldn't move!

Attempts to use my magic failed. He'd blocked me from it. Helpless, I could do nothing to stop him from floating me in his direction. Couldn't stop the man, deity, asshole, who'd been behind the sorrow in my life. And now I'd be a pawn in his sick plot to snare my mother.

A woman who appeared suddenly, her voice soft, her features hidden within the cowl of her cloak. "Unhand my daughter, Prometheus."

The unsurprised bad man half turned to greet her. "Hello, Calliope. I've been waiting a long time for this moment."

"So have I. You and I have a score to settle." My mom pushed back the hood of her cloak, and she looked pretty damned good considering she'd spent thirty years in prison. Even more uncanny, she looked like me minus the pink hair. Hers gleamed a vivid blue, just like her one eye.

"Be careful how you talk to me. I'd hate to hurt your daughter given how long you've been waiting for this reunion."

Mom's lips pressed tight, and her eyes flashed with anger. "You will leave her out of our quarrel."

"Why would I do that when she's living proof you betrayed me?"

"Betrayed you?" Mom uttered a low chuckle. "I was never yours. You might have thought you were winning me over with your gifts, but I saw through you to the dark heart beating in your chest."

"Liar. You would have loved me if not for him."

"Kratos was a thousand times the man you are. The only man I will ever love," my mom declared.

"Is that so? Then why am I bothering to keep your daughter alive? If she's of no use to me, then perhaps I should stick to my original plan. The one where she dies."

The magical fist around me tightened, and I would have gasped if I could breathe. The constriction around my chest stole all air. Spots danced.

Was this how it ended?

"Time for *you* to die." My mom's skin rippled, and blue flames encased her, only for a second before snuffing out. A scream of rage emerged from my mom and Kowalski smirked.

"Did you really think I'd forgotten how to freeze your power? You can't shift or call your flames. Might as well bow to me now."

"Never." Mom held up her hand, and in it, she held a wand. A tiny sliver of wood, but suddenly Kowalski looked uncertain.

"I wouldn't if I were you."

"Why not? It's not as if I have anything to lose. The only thing left for me will be revenge for the husband and daughter you killed."

"I have a different offer for you. Become my wife. My *obedient* wife," he emphasized. "And you and your daughter will live."

"As slaves to your whim," she spat.

"But you'd be together."

The fist on me released suddenly, and I heaved in air before rasping, "Don't do it." I wouldn't see her abase herself for this asshole who'd already cost her so much.

Mom angled her head, and her one blue eye focused on me as she murmured, "I can't lose you after finally finding you."

"Then we need to kill this fucker," I growled.

To which Kowalski-Prometheus laughed. "You can't kill a god."

"But we can hurt it," my mom declared before whipping around her wand and flinging it in his direction. The blast of magic should have decimated the guy. I could see the intensity of it. More power than I could have imagined.

And he didn't even flinch. He held out his arms and let it hit, grinning the whole while. "My turn."

I braced, and so did Mom, but all he did was squish his fingers together.

Snap. The wand broke in half, and Mom blanched.

"I've learned some new tricks while you were away."

Had he? I'd noticed a glint on his finger, one that brightened for a moment when he took on the impact of the blast and again when he used his own power to break the wand. Could the source of his strength be in that piece of jewelry?

How to get it off?

"If I agree to come with you, will you leave my daughter alone?"

"Mommy, no." The name I used to have for her slipped out, and she turned a sad gaze on me.

"I won't see you harmed. You are all that's left of my beloved. The one thing remaining in this world that I love above everything else, even myself."

"I think I'm going to be sick." Prometheus gagged.

"Fuck off, asshole," I growled.

"Is that any way to speak to your soon-to-be stepdaddy?" he mocked.

Blinded with rage and frustration, I ran for him, throwing all my magic in his direction in the form of lances of light while calling on the goddess. *Hekate, I need your help.*

To my surprise, my goddess answered, but not in a way that helped. *Magic won't win this battle. Patience.*

Patience? Was she fucking kidding?

My light arrows hit and were absorbed by Prometheus, who chuckled. "That tickles. My turn now."

His hand, the one with the ring, lifted and pointed. I threw up a hasty shield as my mother screamed, "No! Don't hurt her!"

The gem on his finger lit up, and I braced myself to possibly die.

A shape swooped suddenly from the sky, a snowy white owl that flew in fast and low, and, with a chomp of its beak, severed the finger with the ring.

Prometheus screamed and clutched his hand, spurting blood, to his chest.

The owl landed and shifted into a Kodiak bear that roared in challenge.

Koda had arrived.

CHAPTER 17

The entire flight over, Koda prayed he guessed right about where to go. He'd gotten a strong hint when the ketchup packet burst, but now he had to wonder. It helped that his gut agreed.

As he neared the desolate neighborhood, he saw three people squared off. A head sporting bright blue hair, the chimera. Pink locks, his precious Marissa. And Abe, the demi-god villain. A man he'd once respected.

No more.

Abe held out his hand in Marissa's direction. A glint on it caught Koda's sharp vision. The way it glowed led to him making a split-second decision. He dove as if he were chasing rodents in the field—part of his training in this form. While he didn't usually bite people, he made an exception and sheared off the ring finger.

While Abe made a show of screaming, Koda landed and changed into his most aggressive shape.

The Kodiak bear.

With an adrenaline-charged roar, he hit the ground on four paws and charged Abe while the man wailed about his lost finger. Unfortunately, Abe recovered and spotted Koda coming. He held up a hand, and Koda crashed into an invisible wall. He bounced off it and staggered. He had to blink several times to clear the spots.

Abe advanced on him. "I should have known you'd fall for the girl. The stupid bitch almost had herself killed by Spriggans and all I needed was for someone to come in and keep her alive while I baited her mama. Who knew you'd get so personally invested? Ah well, can't say as I blame you. Like mother, like daughter. They do have a certain something about them."

"Leave him alone," Marissa yelled.

"Or what? Even without the ring of amplification, I'm still stronger." With that taunt, he shot out little lightning bolts that hit Koda and caused him to flinch and writhe.

Marissa threw herself between them, and suddenly, she was the one gasping in pain while Prometheus sneered. "Young love. So willing to sacrifice. Your father was the same. Offering himself up if I promised to leave Calliope alone."

"And you lied. He died for nothing," the woman with blue hair said with a trembling voice.

The attack by Abe stopped, and Marissa trembled

against Koda. He cradled her close in his furry arms wishing he could reassure her.

"I'm sorry," she whispered. "I don't know how to stop him. I thought without the ring we'd have a chance, but he's too powerful."

He was sorry too. Sorry he'd found her only to lose her before they'd had a chance.

"Admit you found it sweet." Prometheus turned to face Calliope though he held a hand up in our direction, maintaining the invisible shield he'd erected. "I followed your every step. I burned down the places you visited so you knew I still cared. And then, as a cherry on top of the sundae, I assigned your daughter to investigate those fires. A gift, an offering, enticing you to approach while I stayed close to her, watching and waiting until you appeared and we could finally be reunited."

"Go to Hell," Calliope spat.

"Are you going to watch your daughter die, or will you finally agree to be my wife?"

The chimera snorted. "We both know I want nothing to do with you, but you leave me no choice. But I will have a binding agreement. One sworn in blood and magic that you will not harm my daughter, her children, or her mate."

"And in return, you will be mine?" Abe stated.

"I will—

"Do no such thing!" boomed a male voice.

A startled Marissa and Calliope whirled to see who spoke, but Koda already knew. Daddy had arrived.

"You're dead!" exclaimed a surprised Abe.

"It will take something nastier than Tartarus to keep me from my wife. Now that I've returned, time to end you once and for all."

Abe smirked. "Ooh, big threats. Do you remember what happened the last time you confronted me?"

Kratos' lips split into a chilling grin. "I do. But what you failed to realize was my time in Tartarus made me strong, and I made a few friends. Many of whom don't like you."

"Did you join together and create a group, Those Outwitted by Prometheus," taunted Abe.

"We did, but our purpose wasn't to complain but to figure out how to take you out." Kratos removed his sword from its sheath, and Marissa sucked in a breath.

"A blade won't be enough," chortled Abe. "And as I recall, you're not that good with fire."

Even before Abe raised his hand to fling any, Calliope inserted herself in front of Kratos. "No. I won't let you take him from me. Not again," she beseeched.

The big man slid an arm around her and murmured, "Fear not, my sweet flower. I am here to stay. But this worm... He's got an invitation to visit Tartarus."

"As if I'd ever go," said a sneering Abe.

"Who said you have a choice? Now!" Kratos yelled.

From behind, two hounds came running, holding a fine filigreed net between them. They swept into Abe, who batted at the strands.

To no avail.

"What is this? Release me," screeched Abe.

Kratos, holding Calliope's hand, stood over the man and had an expression of stone as he said, "Do you like my net? Epimetheus made it special for you. You do remember your brother, right? The one you betrayed. He's looking forward to seeing you again in Tartarus."

"You don't have the power to send me there," stated Abe, and yet he didn't sound entirely certain.

Calliope offered a cold smile as she stood over him and said, "You don't, but with the help of my daughter, I can." She held out her hand to Marissa, who stood and clasped it.

"What do I do?" Marissa murmured.

"Just lend me your strength and I will shape the spell."

Not just Marissa contributed to the casting. The hounds shifted and butted up against her as well, lending some of Hekate's magic.

A low chant emerged from Calliope, and a glow surrounded her. A hazy spot appeared in front of Abe, who struggled anew in his netting.

"Even if you manage to send me, I'll be back," threatened Abe.

"I wouldn't recommend it," Kratos' dry reply.

A swirling dark hole appeared, from which emerged a hot wind. Kratos neared the tangled Abe and reached for the netting.

"You'll regret this."

"No, I won't," the big man stated as he lifted the net and its occupant with ease. With a mighty heave, he sent it soaring through the hole.

The moment Abe disappeared, Marissa's mom stopped chanting. The doorway to Tartarus vanished, and they were left in silence.

And in that quiet, Calliope said, "Dearest husband, I would like you to meet our daughter."

CHAPTER 18

I STARED AT THE BIG MAN WHO WAS SUPPOSED TO BE MY DAD and thought, *Damn he's handsome.* I could see why my mom fell in love.

The look he fixed on me, shocked and yet soft, had me hesitating only a second when he opened his arms and said, "My daughter. I am more happy than you can know to meet you."

The man hugged like a bear, and given I'd just been hugged by Koda the bear, I would know.

Dad lifted me up and murmured, "I will make up the lost years to you."

"I don't need anything." I truly didn't because, in that moment, I was overwhelmed. A mom and a dad in the same day?

Not to mention how Koda came to my rescue. Speaking of which, I glanced at him to see the bear gone. Koda stood looking awkward with his hands shoved in his pockets.

And then he was flanked by two naked hounds in human form. "I've never understood why regular shifters couldn't keep their clothes," he grumbled. "Then again, you also can only do one shape."

"Admit it, big guy, you like us." Orion grinned before adding, "I love a happy ending."

The dour Ambrose even had something nice to say. "Glad we arrived in time."

"How did you even know to come here?" I asked.

"Well, bird boy here went flying off without giving us an address, but Hekate came through," Orion announced with a smug grin.

"Will he really be stuck in Tartarus?" I did kind of worry.

"Even if he did manage to return, we'll be ready. Fear not. He will never harm you or your mother again." Dad squeezed me again before growling. "While your aid was appreciated, hounds, you will clothe yourself around my wife and daughter."

"Yessir." Orion didn't argue just jogged for the car and the trunk where they'd most likely stashed their stuff. Ambrose took his time following, his bare ass flexing.

Koda growled in my direction. "You shouldn't stare."

"Your jealousy is cute, but I'm actually looking at a bit of a problem. That tiny car is not going to fit all six of us," I stated.

"It barely fit three given the dude is huge!" Orion commented as he pulled on a shirt.

"I can fly," Koda stated. "Just tell me where to meet you."

"Might as well use Kowalski's house, seeing as how he won't be needing it." Which reminded me, I'd have to explain everything to the CA. *Hey guys, so you thought you did a great job of cleaning out the corruption in our precinct, and well, you followed up by sending in an evil demi-god. But don't worry, we handled it. Thanks!*

"Guess I'll meet you there, then," Koda stated.

My nose wrinkled. "Pity your owl isn't big enough to carry someone." The idea of being squished between the parents I'd just met—who were currently kissing in a way that might require therapy for me—didn't appeal.

"Actually, I did once meet a griffon hiking in the mountains of the Middle East."

I blinked. "As in flying lion?"

The corner of his mouth quirked. "Nice fellow. Hated visitors but he let me spend the night for a chocolate bar and a good scratch behind the ears."

"Could it handle my weight?"

At his nod, I braced myself and stalked to my parents, who paused in their lip lock to beam at me.

"Baby." My mom sighed my old nickname.

"Hey." Now with the danger done, I found myself shy

"It is my utmost pleasure to meet you, daughter. I look forward to us getting to know one another." Dad had the biggest grin.

"I do too. So, um, given the car is kind of small, Koda's going to give me a ride."

My parents both narrowed their gaze on him, and it was Mom who growled, "What are his intentions?"

Since I doubted me saying "defiling me with an orgasm" would fly, I stuck to, "He's my partner from work. He can be trusted with my life."

Dad nodded. "He is the honorable sort." Then in an aside to Mom, he added, "If he does anything to disrespect or hurt her, I will eviscerate him myself."

Mom beamed. "I'm so happy we get to be a family at last."

The words froze me. A part of me elated, a part of me terrified. What if they hated me? Or I hated them? What if, what if, what if...

As they piled into the car, I returned to Koda, who shifted with a smoothness that I'd never seen from a werewolf. Theirs tended to look a lot more painful.

His griffon had a golden body and snowy white wings, but the eyes remained Koda's. He knelt down so I could swing my leg over his back. His thick mane gave me a handhold, and I needed it as he leaped into the air, which caused me to squeak and hold tight. A little bit of magic kept me in place, and once I realized I wouldn't fall and smush to my death, I enjoyed it.

The night sky was full of stars, and as we flew over the city, the lights provided bright spots. To my surprise, we didn't fly directly to Abe's house but stopped atop an apartment building set up with a rooftop patio.

I slid off his back and, when he shifted, asked, "What's wrong? Why are we stopping?"

Rather than reply, he showed me, dragging me into his arms for the longest kiss.

When it ended, my weak knees meant I had to cling to him to remain upright. "Mmm, what was that for?" I purred.

"For not dying. For standing between me and lightning, and by the way, don't you ever do that again."

"Says the guy who charged a god."

"I realize we haven't known each other long, but—"

I interrupted to say, "Something between us feels right."

"Yeah."

I cupped his cheeks. "Does this mean I can take back what I said about this being casual? Because I am pretty sure we both want more."

"Much more," he agreed before his mouth slanted over mine again.

We made love on that rooftop. Nothing fancy or too long. The kiss resulted in my pants hitting the roof deck and his getting shoved down his thighs.

He hefted me that I might guide him into my sex, already wet and wanting. Our rhythm quick and pleasurable.

Under a sky full of stars, we came together, and in that moment, I knew nothing would ever keep us apart.

Except for my parents.

The moment we walked in, the pair of them were waiting, arms crossed.

"We need to talk, boy," said my dad, putting his arm around Koda and leading him away.

Before I could protest, Mom grabbed my hand and murmured, "He'll be fine. Everything will be fine from now on."

And it was, once we got over a few hiccups, AKA, set boundaries with my parents.

EPILOGUE

Koda found me hiding in the pantry.

"What are you doing?"

"Mshng." My mouthful of chips made it kind of unclear.

He sat down beside me. "What did they do now?"

I swallowed and grimaced. "Threatened to take me to the zoo."

"That doesn't seem so bad."

"It is when you accidentally walked in on them going at it on the couch." I didn't think any amount of bleach would save me from that image.

"In their defense, they have thirty-five years to make up for."

"I know," I groaned. "But couldn't they do it in a bed with the door closed like normal people?"

"They're not normal."

No shit. A chimera for a mom and a demi-god for a dad. "I can't wait until they get their own place."

"How long before the house next door is finished?"

Before anyone laughed at them being so close, it took me having a tantrum before they agreed on separate households because their initial plan was to have me live with them in Abe's house, which I'd been given by the CA as an apology for his actions. Living in the same house? Running into them making out everywhere? Hell to the no.

"The contractor said a month, but I'm pretty sure I can bribe some gnomes to go in at night to hurry up the job."

Koda laughed, a sound that never failed to lighten my mood, but then again, everything about him made me happy. "It won't be long. We'll survive."

"Will we, though?" I whined. I leaned my head on his shoulder. "Pretty sure this wasn't what you signed up for when you asked me to marry you." A marriage proposal that came suspiciously quick after my dad's "talk" with him. Koda swore he did it of his own volition. I had my doubts, but I also knew how much he loved me.

"I don't know. I mean, yeah, your parents are nuts, but I kind of like the way I never know what's going to happen next. Keeps me on my toes."

"Personally, I'd like to never hear again what happens after 'Oh, Big K, give it to me harder.'"

His bark of laughter led to us being discovered. The door to the pantry opened, and my parents stood there looking disheveled but at least wearing clothes.

They beamed at me. "Ready to visit the animals in the zoo?"

Actually, I was. I had my picture taken with the llama. Let my dad buy me all the junk food. I even fed the cute baby goats. As for Koda, he managed to get banned for climbing past some safety enclosures to pet a red panda so he could have it as another shape.

Best day ever!

When we got home, it was to find a pair of visitors.

The giant black dogs lay on the front step, a mangled mail bag between them.

"Not again," I muttered. "You know it's a federal offense to mess with the postal service, right?" I chided.

The pair of hounds lolled their tongues before shifting, which led to my dad bellowing, "Clothes now or I will neuter you both!"

Orion slapped his hands over his junk. "Dude. Chill. We're only staying for a minute. Wanted to let you know we're taking off. Hekate's got a new mission for us."

The goddess had been quiet of late. Then again, I didn't have much need of her now that I had family.

"Where is she sending you now?" I asked.

Ambrose grimaced. "To babysit a human."

"In Canada!" Orion bounced. "Always wanted to ride a moose and sleep in an igloo."

"Sounds like it could be fun."

"I don't like the cold," Ambrose grumbled.

"On that, we agree. Makes my massive penis

turtle," Orion woefully confided, which earned him a growl from both my dad and Koda.

"I'm sure you'll be fine," I soothed.

Famous last words. It appears that Orion and Ambrose are about to go on a wild adventure with a human who will twist them up into knots and challenge their friendship. Will they learn to share the woman they both love? Find out in Earth's Triangle.

www.ingramcontent.com/pod-product-compliance
Lightning Source LLC
LaVergne TN
LVHW031539060526
838200LV00056B/4571